D0686568

SEVENTEEN NAMES FOR
SKIN

ROLAND BLACKBURN

Copyright © 2020 by Roland Blackburn, Artists, Weirdpunk Books

First Edition

WP-0008

All rights reserved.

Cover-wrap art/design by Don Noble

Editing and internal layout/formatting by Sam Richard

Weirdpunk Books logo by Nate Sorenson

All rights reserved.

This is a work of fiction. Names, characters, businesses, places, events, locales, and incidents are either products of the author's imagination or used in a fictitious manner. Any resemblance to actual persons, living or dead, or actual events is purely coincidental.

No part of this book may be reproduced in any form or by any electronic or mechanical mean, including information storage and retrieval systems, except with written permission from the author, except for the use of brief quotations in book reviews.

Weirdpunk Books

www.weirdpunkbooks.com

ALSO BY ROLAND BLACKBURN

Marmalade

The Flesh Molder's Love Song

CONTENTS

FELL

Just before she hired a stranger to kill her, Snow found out that she was going to die.

That in itself was no revelation. She'd known the fact since kindergarten, the way of all flesh and whatever else her Sunday school teachers had quoted back at her while still ducking the hard questions. But that it would come two months shy of her twenty-fourth birthday was hard to believe.

The inevitable was on its way.

Her pasty doctor sat across the desk from Snow, arms folded. A couple of photos blown up into full-sized glossy pages lay between them. In the picture was a skull. In the skull was a spongy mass. And in the mass--

"I'm so sorry," the doctor murmured.

Head ringing, Snow was at a characteristic loss for words. Her eyes kept swinging back to the photos, to the black rose that had lodged itself within her cortex. The malignant bloom that had gorged itself on blood, and now--

"There are treatments," the doctor managed gravely. He was maybe seventy, his wattled skin drooping around a sagging jaw. Snow couldn't remember his name, could barely remember anything now other than the bloody-black tumor lodged smugly at the top of her spine. How could it be that this man would outlive her? "Chemotherapy. Radiation. We can--"

"You said stage four." Her own voice was a whisper, and she hated it. "Are we supposed to count up, or count down? Four's bad, right?"

"I'm not going to lie to you. " A pained crease pulled across his forehead.

"How long?"

"It's bad. But--"

"How long?" The next time it came out cleaner. "How long do I have?"

"It's not an exact science, but--" The doctor looked down at his notes again, happy to break eye contact. "Six months. If that. But there are treatments---"

"Of course. What are my chances?"

"It's not that simple."

Of course it is. Snow remembered visiting the zoo as a child, with her father pointing out the rarer animals, helpful signs outside the habitats pointing out how many were left in the world, how many years they may have left until extinction. If they could calculate that, a headcount and a funeral dirge, surely they could tell a longshoreman's daughter how long she had left.

What is he going to do?

"Try me. Run the numbers."

His sagging mouth sank deeper into a frown. "Five percent."

Snow drummed her fingers on the desk, hard enough to chip paint. *Ice up, Snow.* "Radiation. Chemicals. I'm guessing the side effects would be excruciating?"

"We're not barbarians, Ms. Turner. Medicine has come a

long way." The doctor folded his hands and leaned away from her. "But, yes. There would be quite a lot of discomfort involved. And the monetary cost--"

Snow had already spent money she didn't have just to get the tests done.

Damn Raven for pushing me into this. I could have just dropped dead in peace.

But a dark kernel began to form in her mind. Snow thought of her father in the vintage wheelchair, the oxygen tank always tucked behind it. She thought of him evicted, then out on the street. Before long he'd be sharing her plot.

She didn't have six months.

At that moment, Snow knew it.

"Can I ask you a question?"

A little wary, the pasty man nodded.

"What would you do?" Snow leaned forward, locking her eyes with his. "It's you with the tumor. Your choice. What would the medical professional's move be here?"

"Me?" The doctor's eyebrows went up comically. It made his pasty white face seem less hateful in that second, almost jovial, and she almost forgave him his capacity for survival. "I'd surround myself with the people I loved, and love them all I could."

✳

"WHAT'S THE MATTER WITH YOU! YOU LOOK LIKE SHIT!"

Raven almost had to scream it in her ear, her plastic cup dangerously close to spilling onto her shoes. Peter Murphy was thudding from the speakers over some new spook-house remix, and not for the first time Snow thought Hedge's Halloween party might have been a poor choice for her last night on earth. But this had been the only public gathering she could think of, so she had to stick to it.

She didn't have another two grand to spend on murder.

Snow had stopped by her father's trailer that afternoon, groceries and Talbot in hand. He'd looked tired, but happy to see her, and they'd run down each other's goings-on with cheerful aplomb, Snow trying all the while not to cry. It was her financial support supplementing his meager pension that was keeping him in rent and food, and without her, she thought he'd be forced out on the street soon enough. He'd asked about her band (*the loudest in Portland*), romantic life (*non-existent*), and her future (*six months and ticking down*) before telling her he loved her and just wanted to see her happy.

The dark kernel of a plan had unfurled its roots, and she'd watered it eagerly.

If you were going to die anyway, why not help the ones you love?

Obtaining the life insurance itself had been surprisingly easy. She'd found a policy online, fired a couple of emails back and forth, and had signed on the dotted line within twenty-four hours, with an additional endorsement added for a double payout in case she was the victim of a violent crime. There was no shortage of corporations willing to roll the dice on a young woman in the picture of health.

The hardest part, though, was actually getting herself killed. Suicide was right out as it would invalidate the policy, and Snow didn't know any contract killers. Nor was she clear on how to find one. Trolling through the back booths of dive bars seemed like the way to go, but starting up that many conversations with strangers would be enough to do her in even if drowning herself in Rainier didn't. Were someone to take her up on the offer, Snow didn't think she could handle the embarrassment when they opened the envelope, turned over the picture of the victim-to-be, and muttered "Youse? You want me to kill youse?"

The anxiety of soliciting her own death in public and the ensuing awkward conversation were almost enough to make her give up on her own murder entirely. Snow was looking at pictures of bridges to be pushed off of when she remembered some soundbite about a criminal underworld lurking on the dark web.

The TOR browser had been easy enough to upload. The problem, though, was that using it wasn't exactly as advertised. No one tried to push oxycontin on her, or hire her as a drug mule, or solicit her for snuff films. Instead, the dark web was like being in an orgy with the lights off. Something was going on, but she was damned if she could find it.

She'd tried cross-referencing dark web-links off of Reddit for most of forty-eight hours. She'd sat in cryptic one-topic chat rooms, spurned webcam offers, and batted away cryptocurrency ploys by the handful. Losing hope, she'd finally struck up a conversation with someone tagged *inceLL666* who hinted that they might know someone who might know someone that could help her. Snow had tried to fish around for more details, realizing that this could be a real Nigerian prince situation and that she might not have thought this through all the way, but *inceLL666* followed up by saying that they were local Portlanders, could provide a long history of misanthropic violence, and, most importantly, had set up and delivered half a dozen contracts in the last year alone.

They'd even offered to throw in references.

Even though she wasn't the most discriminate criminal mastermind, Snow had no illusions about how sketchy this guy was. But who else could she find to do the job?

Worse, what if the time bomb in her head went off before she could?

Impetuous as it was, she'd gone ahead and jumped off the bridge. Concocting some story about how Samantha "Snow" Turner had wronged her, (*that betch*, he'd typed) she supplied some vital facts and an old, slightly unflattering photo to the maniac on the other end's email. *inceLL666* replied almost instantly, letting her know they had agreed upon terms and needed a week to put it together, along with a prospective time and place.

Satisfied, Snow told them about Hedge's Halloween party.

The anonymous user wanted two grand, the amount a deep discount for a slighted brother, which she found frankly offensive. After a moment's hesitation, she'd transferred over a large chunk of her savings, not sure if murder for hire was the kind of thing one was supposed to haggle over. Honestly, she'd expected her life to be worth more.

Snow added only one condition. *Burn the body.*

✳

"You okay, Snow?" Raven gave her a shake that rattled her teeth. If there was one thing you could say about Raven, it was that she was all about tough love.

Straightening, Snow gave her friend a thousand-watt smile as if she hadn't been scanning the faces in the room for her murderer and rubbed her little terrier Talbot behind the ears. The idea of her dog starving to death undiscovered in her apartment had plagued her all afternoon until she'd just decided to bring him along, figuring someone would rescue him at the scene. "I was up late! Haven't been sleeping well lately!"

"Yeah!" Raven waggled her eyebrows, her pink pigtails bobbing in time with the beat. With her raccoon mascara, she looked a little like a magician's assistant. "Getting some thunder up in that cemetery, is that it? I thought you were picky!"

Snow rolled her eyes. "I'm not picky. I hate intimacy."

"The problem is that you never relax. Get comfy in that

skin, bitch!" The raccoon punk flicked at the silver piercings that dotted both of Snow's ears, the two-inch spike cresting through the ridge of her helix, and the little ring through her nose. "You're cramming metal through people's intimate parts on a daily basis, Snow. How much closer do you have to get?"

Snow tried to swat her away, but Raven was nothing if not persistent. Before she could gain any leverage, Marquette swooped in, a plastic goblet spilling over in each hand. People told Snow that she was a little tall for a woman, but Marquette was tall for a power forward, an Amazon with shoulders like a linebacker. In high school, she'd been an all-state safety, the rumor went, but had traded that in for heels and now fronted a punk band called Clit Commander that played a couple of shows a week in the seedier parts of town. Snow and Raven had opened for them a handful of times at the Coma Lounge in their on-again/off-again effort to get their act Bleeding Facelift, Portland's loudest band, off the ground.

"Ladies!" Marquette tried not to slosh Hawaiian Punch and Caribbean rum over the both of them as she swept the pair up in a bone-crushing hug. Raven recoiled with a hiss, but Snow allowed herself to get drenched.

It wasn't like she was going to be wearing these clothes again.

"What are you supposed to be, bitch?" Raven almost had to scream it.

Marquette rolled a hand down her billowing pink pillbox suit. "Giant Jackie O. It hurts that you have to ask. What are you, Snow White?"

Snow had barely bothered a costume at all. All in black, her only concessions were to be even whiter than usual and hollow out her eyes a little. "Sexy ghost."

"You?" Marquette tilted the goblet Raven's way, who almost slapped it out of her hand.

"THIS--IS NOT--A COSTUME!" Raven clapped her hands to her leather vest and chains over a Dead Kennedys t-shirt. "Stop sloshing that shit on me. People'll think I started drinking."

"Well, ladies, I'm an ever-turning gear on the rumor mill." Gesturing with her goblet, the big woman threw an elbow that almost capsized Snow. "There's a tasty piece of chicken who's been giving Ms. White the eye. Take a gander in the direction of yonder Tall Man."

For a moment Snow had no idea what she was talking about. With another brutal nudge, she was directed to an immaculate velvet painting of Angus Scrimm in *Phantasm*, his undertaker's suit a rich midnight black and a shiny sphere clutched in one upraised palm. Below it was a cute redhead talking to Hedge, who was probably wouldn't shut up about Simon and Garfunkel.

"Who, Phantasm?" Raven yelled.

Before Snow could complete her once-over, Phantasm glanced her way, and Snow quickly recoiled into her red plastic cup. She didn't look like a murderer, but maybe that was Snow just being biased.

Those eyes, though. A piercing green, so sharp it was dangerous.

But she wasn't there to meet new people.

Snow had come there to die.

"Get over there!" Raven howled it in her ear. "Bitch, get some thunder up in that cemetery!"

"Will you stop?" Snow hissed back.

Raven started grinding against her hip until Marquette pulled her off. Pouring some of her goblet into Snow's glass, her voice was low and husky "I'm just the messenger, honey. You do you."

Shaking her head, Snow took a sip and found the mixture not half bad, even though she'd always hated coconut. It was at least a distraction from the redhead, who to be fair may or may not have been planning to kill her. Snow's last fling had been half a decade ago, an emotionally scarring power trip that she'd considered herself lucky to have gotten out of in one piece. Since then, she'd approached romance with the same attitude reserved for dictators, demagogues, and dogfighters.

As Raven would have put it, the cemetery had been locked up for some time.

Before too long, though, she was pleasantly buzzed and swaying vaguely to the reverberating bass crushing the walls. Thoughts drifting, Snow began to wonder if she should have specified her manner of death. Was that an option?

Flaming chainsaws, acid dissolutions, or piano wire were probably not high on any contract killer's list, but none of them had ever been officially taken off the table.

Maybe the dark bloom was already corrupting her thoughts. Forcing her fists open, Snow tried to relax. It would all be over soon.

Except it wasn't. People floated in and out of conversations, old faces mixing with the new for hours. Before long, Snow wondered if she hadn't just thrown her money in a blender.

How could you have been so stupid?

She began to revisit accidents in her mind. Falling off a bridge? Stepping off the curb in front of a bus? With her recent turn of luck, no doubt she'd suddenly turn invulnerable.

Her father would need the money when she was gone. She had to figure something out.

She thought, and thought, and thought.

And waited for the blow to come.

❋

THE THREE OF THEM STUMBLED DOWN THE SIDEWALK, Marquette draping her big hands over their shoulders as they passed beneath yellow streetlights and through deep patches of shadow, Talbot trailing behind. Brick buildings and old stucco storefronts drifted by on the abandoned streets beneath the light of a full moon, relics eighty years old in a neighborhood that was rife with urban renewal. Their surroundings were as silent as spirits, and Snow knew that in ten years there would be nothing left but condos and high-rise apartments.

She wouldn't be around to see it.

An autumnal chill dampened the air, and Snow found herself wishing that she'd dressed a little warmer. If she died of frostbite, though, she was pretty sure her father stood to collect half.

Aware that perhaps her murderer was only waiting to separate her from the pack, Snow had tried to walk home alone, but the other two wouldn't hear of it. Instead, they chanted Misfits songs off-key and tried not to trip over cracks in the sidewalk as they slalomed along the pavement.

After the first ten blocks, Raven deposited herself cheerfully at the stoop of a squat brownstone apartment. She'd buzzed in through the front door and was about to hurry up the stairs with a wave when Snow hugged her. The embrace was long and crushing.

"Love you," she whispered. "You're my best friend."

"Love you too, bitch. You sure you're okay?" A slight frown creased her forehead, and Raven gave her a once-over with raccoon eyes. "Did you ever get out to see that doctor?"

Snow nodded. For a moment, the raccoon punk looked like she might say something else, but then just bounded away. Snow wondered if it would be the last time she'd ever see her.

Marquette escorted her down the empty boulevard, Talbot trotting along beside them and sniffing at objects of skeptical interest. She kept the chatter idle with talk of bands they'd seen, bands they hated. Snow kept trying to peel Marquette off, to get Marquette to go a different route on the off chance that she hadn't just flushed two grand down the toilet, but the big woman wasn't buying it. She'd had crushes that were less clingy.

It wasn't until they'd gone a couple of blocks that Marquette put a massive palm on her shoulder and grunted. "Someone's behind us. Be cool."

Snow was about to turn but instead looked in the plate glass window of a used instrument store. Someone was indeed about thirty paces back, wearing a white sheet with ragged black holes cut out for eyes. A refugee from a Halloween party, no doubt, stumbling towards home.

But her heart quickened all the same.

Had they been at Hedge's?

She tried to cycle through her memories, but the night was full of blurred faces and too much of whatever the hell Marquette had kept pouring into her plastic cup. Besides, the sheet was forgettable enough to simply slip past the eye, an ancient relic beneath notice that even now was drifting through the night towards them.

It could hide anything.

The thought slapped her awake, and she risked another glance back over her shoulder. The ghost hadn't veered off at the last intersection but instead maintained its distance, hovering above the sidewalk. The folds billowed in the east wind, and Snow couldn't make out any unnatural bulges. Nothing to indicate that the stranger was armed.

Nothing to indicate that they weren't.

Despite herself, Snow began to walk faster. Part of her wanted to slow down, to let the plan run its course. If this was somehow her delayed killer, wasn't this what she'd paid for?

But there were other ways to get her father money, enough to keep him in the medication his pension couldn't. Other ways that didn't involve her bleeding out on a forgotten section of concrete, dying on a street she couldn't name.

Marquette cursed and struggled to keep up. Her size fourteens hadn't been built for speed. "You know that guy?"

Snow shook her head and risked another glance back. The bedsheet ghost was drawing closer, twenty-five paces now, then twenty, excess fabric rippling in the breeze. Whoever was beneath the cloth was tall, broad-shouldered. Deep pits where their eyes should be echoed blankly into hers. The dark ring of the thing's mouth yawned.

Snow scooped up her dog and tried to move faster, willing herself to not collapse into an all-out sprint. Talbot whined. Despite her morbid preoccupation over the last week, maybe she could try the chemo. The drugs. Maybe she just wasn't ready to die.

Had she done everything she'd ever wanted, or had she just wasted her time in this suit of flesh? How many times had she let her fear get in the way?

Maybe she should have embraced it all.

She had a feeling that she wasn't going to get to find out.

Reaching the corner of the next building, Snow glanced behind her.

She froze.

The sheet was just dead laundry, roiling empty upon the sidewalk behind them.

Nothing was inside it.

Nothing moved.

Snow turned, this time breaking into a run.

Then the night exploded around her.

Something heavy burst out of the alley, a wet, hot thing passing mere inches from her face. It reeked of melted iron as it hit her across the chest with the speed of a falling anvil. If she hadn't flinched at the last second, it would have taken her at the throat. As it was, the impact knocked on her ass and sent her spinning.

Her forehead connected with the pavement, and for a moment a constellation of white stars waltzed before her. Hot pain lanced through her shoulder and scalp. As she struggled to sit up, her hand came away sticky.

Did something just bite me?

Marquette was yelling something, fists balled, circling around to her front. Talbot scampered closer and licked her palm. Snow rose into a crouch, ignoring the pain in her tailbone and left ear. The spike bounced loosely against her temple, barely holding on by a flap of skin.

Damn thing almost ripped my ear off.

Marquette darted to one side and, for the first time, Snow could see it. The thing was on all fours, massive, with a leering, canine face and ridiculous tufted ears, too oversized for its elongated skull. It was covered in brownish-grey fur, a bushy tail rigid and taut over muscular haunches.

Every now and again she'd seen coyotes in Portland, lone stragglers from the trails and nature preserves that sluiced through the town like capillaries. But this thing was maybe three times the size of one, a bulky monstrosity the size of a small pony.

The coyote-thing snarled, ropes of saliva dripping from its distended jaw. It focused its amber eyes on hers, trembling with rage or spent energy or both.

Marquette then kicked it square in the face. She might have been dressed like Jackie O, but she was still wearing steel-toed Doc Martens, and the thing squealed with pain as Snow struggled to find her feet.

White lights swam before her eyes, and Snow wondered how badly she was bleeding. She willed Talbot to run, but looking back, she realized something must have happened to him too.

Her terrier lay whimpering in the gutter between the sidewalk and the street, a ragged cut in his side, wet and black beneath the amber lights. His breath was shallow and panting, and her heart sank.

No. No. No. No.

The thing leapt at Marquette again, and this time the sinewy woman couldn't dodge it. The collision sounded like an axe splitting dead wood as it planted both its forelegs in her chest. They collided with the pavement, the thing's bulk pinning her arms. Triumphant, it sank its jaws down upon her throat.

Her scream became a wet gurgle.

Absently, Snow patted at the burning pain that had been her left ear. Her hand came away wet and slippery, the hole where it had been had torn wide open, exposing cartilage. The spike slid out of the gap without the least resistance. She could smell copper on the air, feel her own sodden clothes clinging to her, a chill starting to take command that made her fingers numb and racked shivers all the way down her spine.

Planting the spike between her knuckles, Snow took a step forward, then another. The coyote-thing had its snout buried in the ruined throat of Marquette, squatting in the middle of a sprawling puddle. Whatever its original intent, it seemed to have forgotten all about her to scarf down dark delicacies.

It took Snow nothing to step in front of it. Nothing to drive the silver all the way through its eye.

With the swing of one massive paw, the howling coyote-thing struck her. Fresh, scorching pain drew fiery lines across her chest as it sent her careening into a telephone pole.

Her head struck the thick wood. Everything greyed out for a moment.

She had time to watch the coyote-thing collapse.

Before she gave up the ghost and the darkness took her, Snow thought she saw it change.

MEMBRANE

The room was cold. She couldn't breathe.

Snow had been drifting in and out of a dream, thoughts of yellow-green forests and sunshine, her body bobbing instinctually across empty fields. Floating on gossamer wings, she would land on mammoth flowers, each bright as a sunburst with fiery reds and yellows, and lower her proboscis to sup on sweet ambrosia--

But there was something off here, and when she struggled to right herself, she knew that she wasn't in her own bed. Something was horribly wrong with her, some massive and clinging mask draped across her face.

And then the sheet of ice engulfed her.

Freezing chills scored her flesh, complex storms reverberating in numbing flares throughout her spine. Something behemoth slipped between her shoulders. Her forehead and jaw began to ache unmercifully, and agony opened up across her ribs, her hips. Even the cold itself hurt, the sensation of burning more intense than the real thing, but after a few moments she could feel her fingers again, her lips, her legs beneath her.

Snow opened her eyes.

The material that surrounded her was a fibrous milky green. Daylight filtered through it weakly, and Snow could feel it behind and below her as well, the material not entirely unpleasant against her bare flesh. The fabric was all around her, wrapping her in a puke-colored sleeping bag.

With an attempted swipe from her unfamiliar arm, Snow found that she couldn't move.

Real panic began to set in. Beyond her entombment, Snow realized that she had no idea where she was. Who might have taken her? Memories of the previous night began to come drifting back, technicolor-clear.

The coyote-thing.

Marquette, gurgling her life out onto the sidewalk.

Poor Talbot, the gaping wound in his side as he lay panting in the wet gutter.

And now she was imprisoned.

Other memories came floating back: the shredded ruin of her helix, the deep gouges the thing's teeth had left in her collarbone, her lifeblood pouring out as she drove the needle through the chimera's eye, but those were physical and inconsequential things, pieces of a jigsaw to be sorted out as soon as the current crisis was averted.

She pressed against the spun material. Practical nails slipped and skittered across the woven threads. Snow thought she felt something give.

Repeating the process now with the other hand, she pushed harder with her wrists, fingers clenching and unclenching. More fibers began to snap.

Her breath came in hot wet puffs against the material that clung to her face. Never a fan of tight spaces, she was willing herself not to cry, not to think about Marquette or little Talbot, only to escape this trap in which she'd awoken.

And then get revenge. Oh, there was a sweet kernel of poison there, as well.

Any thoughts of dying now were gone.

Her fingers broke through the husk, savoring the rush of clean, cool air that swarmed across them. Snow pressed now with her forearms, clawing at the threads encasing her torso, her thighs, ripping chunks out wherever she could. The shroud began to fall away, piece after shredded piece, until she could move both arms.

Snow worked at the spun cloth with a fury, ripping it from her chest, then finally off her face. Sunlight struck her like a dirty secret, filtering in through the blinds of a room she barely recognized, and she breathed in gasps of sweet, pure air.

Kicking free from the last of her encasement, Snow fell.

It wasn't a long fall, but those are often the worst. Her collision with the carpet rattled her head with a thump across the floorboards, but on impulse she was back on her feet in a heartbeat, ready to fight, ready to kill if she had to.

She stood nude in the center of a small bedroom, which looked for all the world like someone's low-rent apartment.

Then Snow recognized it.

Of course she did.

It was hers.

❇

EVERY FEATURE OF THE ROOM HAD HER STAMP UPON IT. THE thrift-store mattress. The second-hand drawing table she kept propped against one wall. The scarred and battered bureau that squatted half-in, half-out of the mirrored closet.

Snow caught a glimpse of herself in the lone surviving door and marveled. Only thin white lines marked her from collarbone to breast, a far cry from the gaping holes the coyote-thing's teeth had gouged. As she turned her head and pushed back an ebony lock, her ear was likewise somehow none the worse for wear.

From the resultant damage, the whole nightmare could have been just that. A dream.

But her body gave lie to any such thoughts. She was still covered with dried blood, a long dirty smear that began at her shoulder, curved down her breast, painted her hips, and slipped down her thigh.

Snow pivoted away from the mirror, only to have something else catch her eye.

In the far corner of the ceiling was an identical green bag-

--cocoon--

--to the one she'd bullied her way out of moments before. Glancing over her shoulder, she studied the ruined sack, burst and exposed with frayed strings. Part of her couldn't believe that she'd been trapped inside it only moments ago.

Part of her wondered what was in the other one.

The ruptured casing took up most of the wall over the bed and a good portion of the ceiling. The smaller one was almost an adorable miniature of hers, maybe three feet by two feet of milky-green splayed threads.

She fancied she could hear noises.

Reaching beneath the mattress, Snow grabbed her knife. It wasn't much in the way of home protection, but the four inches of carbide steel felt good in her hand as she pulled the worn chair out from her drawing table and propped it below the far corner of the room. Boosting herself up on either side of its rickety frame, she became aware of the open window, how good the air felt circulating against her. It was as if forgotten neurons had flared back into life, and parts of her were now awash in long sequestered sensations.

Bracing herself against the wall with one free hand, she

took the other and delicately pressed the tip of the steel into the top of the--

--cocoon, impossible but just call it what it is already--

--bag, and drew it down. A gentle pressure, then the blade tugged downward, strands parting with silvery ease.

A familiar whine.

Working faster, Snow cut horizontally across the threads, trying to ignore the slick organic feel against her fingertips. It was not unlike cutting hair.

A little paw emerged from the cloth. A hot, wet tongue stroked the back of her hand.

She lifted Talbot out of the torn mass, already cooing sweet nonsense to her little pup. He wagged his tail furiously, and for the moment she let his needs overtake her own.

The night before, she'd lost him.

And now here he was, miraculously intact.

She turned him this way and that. Her last memories had been of him torn open, dying in the gutter.

There wasn't a scratch on him. Just the faintest hint of a white stripe along his side.

Throwing on an oversized t-shirt, Snow wandered out into the tiny kitchen and threw kibble and wet food together into his dish before setting it on the floor. Talbot dug in as if he hadn't eaten in weeks.

Even the smell of his admittedly unpleasant dog food sent shockwaves of hunger quaking through her stomach.

When was the last time she'd eaten?

She was about to find a snack when her phone's chirp pierced the air.

The sound was a foreign alarm, so alien to her that for a moment she couldn't place it. Glancing around the room, she tried to source out the sound, but with the intermittent chirping she couldn't quite locate her cell.

There was a knock on the door.

Snow froze, torn between the sudden pangs of hunger, annoyance at the phone, and now this. The knock came again, this time a trifle more insistent.

Treading as lightly as she could and bumping her bare ass gracelessly into the counter, Snow crept over to stare out of the peephole.

Two middle-aged men in wrinkled suits stood on her doorstep, glancing around. The mustached one had a paper cup from Juliani's Deli on the first floor, sipping his fountain drink as his bald partner tried not to fall asleep on his feet. They looked like they were competing to see which of them could become the most disheveled, and the way both of them glanced around every couple of seconds emitted a kind of wary authority she could feel even through the door.

Cops.

The bald one hammered on the door again, and the mustached one mouthed something at him from around his straw.

Without thinking, she cracked open the door.

The bald cop looked surprised, as if he hadn't expected a response and had no idea what to do now that he'd gotten one. The mustached cop smiled and slurped down more of his soda. Snow recognized the look and then realized that she was wearing only the oversized pajama shirt.

Fucking hell. Where's your head at?

At least the hem of the shirt drooped low enough to cover the bloodstain. Or so she hoped.

Snow recovered, put on her ice-queen deadpan, and stared back. "Hey."

The mustached cop nodded and flapped open a leather case with a shining star inside it as if it would mean anything to her. "Detective Pachowski. This hirsutely-challenged gentleman is Detective Mgbeke. We were hoping to ask you a couple of questions."

They must have had lunch before coming up because they smelled amazing. Garlic and pepper and sweet, horrible cold cuts wafted in and out of her nostrils, mustard and mayonnaise and bell peppers, and she felt the pang of hunger this time like a sharp kick to the stomach. Snow was starving. If either man had been a sandwich, she would have devoured them whole. "Yeah?"

Mgbeke looked down for a moment and then rocketed his eyes back up. His gaze was being gravitationally drawn to her bare legs. "Mm--did you want to put something else on?"

"It's my house. I'll dress how I want, thanks." It was the exact opposite of how she felt, but it was out before she could stop it. Her dad had taught her from age five onward not to talk to the police, and enmity fought her mouth for dominance. The wiser part of her mind was urging her to shut the fuck up while she was still covered in blood, but this morning the channels had become more than a little confused.

"Your call. Can't say I mind, little lady." Pachowski looked down again, a leather notebook appearing in one hand, but Snow had the feeling he was seizing another opportunity to ogle her from the waist down. He perked up at the electronic chirping of her phone in the background, now locked in some kind of on-again, off-again cycle. "You want to get that?"

"Robocallers."

He shrugged. "No wonder you haven't picked up the phone. Would have made this easier."

"I haven't been feeling well." It seemed the least confrontational under the circumstances.

"Did you know Denis Washington, Ms. Turner?"

The name didn't ring any bells. Her stomach rumbled again, her mouth growing wet with saliva. "Who?"

Mgbeke raised an eyebrow. It seemed the sole gesture in

his facial repartee. "Also went by the stage name Marquette Sinner?"

"Big girl? Fronts a punk band?" Pachowski chimed in, slurping from his soda.

Marquette. Snow hadn't known her real name.

She kept her face frozen while her mind raced, a trick her dad had taught her as a byproduct of his not-so-legal video bootlegging business run out of their garage. Snow knew she was guiltless, but if that was a salvation the prisons would be empty.

--why are they here what do they have?--

"Front-*ed.* Washington was found dead two days ago in the heart of the Belmont district. You know anything about it?" Pachowski took another long swig from his cup.

The shock must have showed, but it was mostly at the brusque manner in which the detective cast her friend's death at her without comfort or cushion. *Two days?* "She's dead?"

Mgbeke gave his partner a look that was either disgust or amazement. "Your friend was the victim of an apparent robbery gone bad."

Pachowski shot Mgbeke a look that could have caused his immolation. "You were at a party together, correct? Witnesses saw you leaving with a--" he checked the note-book again. "--Ms. De La Cruz?"

He said Raven's name as if it was all one word. The raccoon punk would have kneed him in the balls, cop or no cop, but Snow remained expressionless. She could feel the heat burning in her cheeks, her eyes growing wet. The thought of taking a nice, garlicky bite out of the mustached detective was starting to appeal to her.

Despite her better judgment, Snow gave a brief, fabri-cated, but ironclad version in which she and Marquette had parted ways a few blocks after Raven had left them. She had no idea where Marquette had lived, but didn't feel the fact could contradict her story. Mgbeke nodded as Pachowski scribbled, frowned, and stole glances at her pale toned thighs.

They didn't try to contradict her. In turn, she kept everything as brief and vague as possible, knowing that this was only their first pass.

Finally, Pachowski put the pad away. "What do you do for a living, Ms. Turner?"

"I'm a piercer." She didn't mention her drawings, the freelance art projects that sometimes paid enough for coffee on the side. Snow could almost hear her father's voice in her head.

Volunteer nothing.

Mgbeke nodded. There was something in it she didn't like.

Pachowski grinned. "Huh. In my experience, most of those people can't keep from practicing on themselves. Whole bunch of holes. Here, there, everywhere a hole-o."

His eyes dropped for the briefest instant before they met hers again. There was something mocking in it, some *I-know-something-you-don't-know* that Snow dreaded. She could have torn his throat out. "Yet look at you. No jewelry. No piercings. Nary a hole on you, kid."

INTEGUMENT

S till ravenous, Snow pulled into the parking lot of
Inktropolis with the stench of burning rubber close
behind. It may have been the tires of the old Corolla, or
maybe a melting hose in the engine. She wasn't sure, and that
morning out of all others, couldn't care less.

After the detectives had left, Snow had rushed into the
bathroom, torn off her t-shirt, and looked again.

Her jewelry was gone, though she'd find it later the next
morning, interwoven in the strands of her cocoon. Her face
was as silky smooth as it had been at twelve. Her nipples
were somehow unmarked. No scars. No holes.

No indication that needles had ever touched her.

With a growl, she threw herself in the shower and let the
scalding water hit her full in the face. Only when the blood
began to come off in ragged patches did she feel everything
rising to the surface. Her grief, her guilt, her confusion all
bubbled together in a terrible cauldron, and she let herself
cry then, just for a moment.

But this time it wouldn't stop on command. If she hadn't
wanted to die, to set her ailing father up before she went off

howling into the void, none of this might have happened. That the internet prick probably wasn't also a monster coyote but had just pocketed her two grand was of no consolation. Somehow her desire to die had brought this down upon them.

Without it, Marquette would still be alive.

When Snow had pulled herself together, her skin pink and stinging from the heat, she toweled off, threw on an old Dirty Hessian Debacle t-shirt, black jeans, and spider-red Chucks, then went about the long, slow process of hunting for her cell phone. Eventually, she tracked down the intermittent chirping, which was both too grating and too random to be of any help to her finding it, and checked her messages.

The incessant beeps had been her scheduling app. Snow was running ten minutes late for a follow-up appointment with Dr. Pasty, and on her current pace she would be insanely late to Inktropolis. Tempted to blow off the doctor entirely, she made a flurry of calls, the first one to her employer. Duke, a burly bald man with a long goatee and more ink than Shakespeare, cursed her out for an uncharacteristic two minutes, thanks to her no-show the day before. After a moment's finagling and some mild stretching of the truth, he finally agreed that she could push her appointments back.

"Barely. Just *barely.*"

She almost told him that she was dying, if only to get him to park the guilt trip, but finally thanked him, hung up, and called the doctor's office. The office was behind schedule anyway, so if she could get there *right now* they could still draw some blood and run some lab work for her.

It was just after eleven when Snow, now ravenous, was able to reach the parlor. Duke, who was tattooing a starfish on a pretty blonde's calf, barely gave her a conciliatory nod as she rushed into her workspace. Glancing around for donuts in the vague hope that today was one of the random mornings where Duke's generosity had overflowed, she found herself alternately setting up her gear and wolfing down the two energy bars she'd kept in her purse as emergency snacks.

Her first gig of the day was a septum piercing on a twenty-year-old. The second was a conch on a cheerleader she had to card. Settling into a familiar rhythm, she started to calm down, feeling the familiar coldness begin to take hold. Clean the flesh, sterilize the equipment. Inhale, center herself, and then run them through with tenderness.

There was a brusque intimacy to it that she enjoyed, the businesslike nature even when threading a needle through someone's most sensitive parts. It helped her keep her own wandering flesh at bay, satisfy some need in her for closeness that she couldn't quite define. Here was a physical rapport that even their loved ones could never share, a connection through trauma that fulfilled everyone involved. Pierced eyebrows, cock rings, indents, and mods. Everyone was looking to be different, if only in the same ways.

But by three, it wasn't that Snow had started to get hungry again so much as that she'd lurched into starvation. She was looking for a break in the action, something that could let her disappear to the Surf Taco next door or the Murder Pie on the other end of the strip mall for fifteen minutes. The pangs were starting to intensify, making her fingers a little jittery, and she swiped a soda from Duke's mini-fridge if only to let the sugar serve directly as emergency fuel in the meantime.

When the bald man wandered in, causing the little bell on the door to chime, any thoughts of a snack went quickly by the wayside.

Snow could smell trouble. It radiated off of him like bad aftershave.

The bald man's only concession to hair was a patchy dark oval goatee that looked as if he'd put his tongue in an exhaust pipe. He was tall and the wrong kind of bulky, a broadness of muscle slowly atrophying into fat, and beneath his colossal forehead the man's beady eyes marked her the moment he stalked into the lobby.

Duke was on a brief respite at the front desk, sketching out a hobgoblin peeking out from beneath a haunted tree on transfer paper. He gave the guy a once-over and a brief smile. Both of them looked like they could be meeting in a federal prison yard, but Snow also knew that Duke played dungeon master twice a week and could outline the step by step process of deck-building mechanics in at least half a dozen different games she'd never heard of. If he'd ever been in a fight, it had been over the proper turn order in Lords of Waterdeep.

The bald man, on the other hand, looked like the kind of guy who'd dump beer on opposing fans at football games, then jump them with his friends in the men's room. He sidled up to the counter, taking in his surroundings with an obnoxious languor, and dropped both elbows onto it. A black *LL* against a dark sunburst was emblazoned on the back of his left forearm.

"Hey." Duke glanced up again, appraised the artwork with cool disdain, and nodded. If he had noticed the stranger trying to cram into his personal space, it had no effect, and he slid the paper smoothly away. "What can I do for you?"

The bald man nodded back to the booths, and Snow realized the stranger was looking right at her. It came to her that the only thing standing between her and him was a swinging half-door that might just hit him at the knees.

"I want a tattoo." The bald man stared her down.

Duke didn't blink. To be fair, the man's style and etiquette were on par for about thirty percent of their walk-in crowd, so the fact that no alarm bells had started ringing in Duke's head was something she could hardly fault him for. "Cool. As it happens, I do tattoos. What do you want?"

"Her." The big man gestured back to Snow. She took a swig of the soda, finishing almost half the can. The sugar and caffeine were helping, but she still felt jittery, uncomfortable in her own skin. Snow despised the feeling. "I want her to do it."

"She's not a tattoo artist." Duke's smile was slowly fading.

"What does she do?"

"Piercings."

"I want that." The bald man's eyes locked upon Snow again, and he grinned. Unwilling to be cowed, she forced herself up to the front of the room and propped her elbows up on the desk, an imitation of the bald man's pose, resting the can of soda next to Duke's elbow.

"Are we going to have a problem here?" The humor had gone out of Duke's voice, a vague unease of menace now taking up residence.

"This is a business, right? Then let's do business." The stranger focused his attention on Snow as if Duke had suddenly left the room. "I want a spike. Just like the one you had in your ear."

Snow had to force her fingers away from the spot. She'd kept her hair down that morning, hoping Duke wouldn't notice the sudden absence of more than a dozen piercings and their corroborating holes, but now a cold ember ignited somewhere below the pit of her stomach. "What?"

"Been a little blue lately? Bitch?"

"Get the fuck out of my store," Duke said it as if giving out the time of day. Snow didn't have to look down to see his fingers had curled around the handle of the Louisville

Slugger tucked behind the counter. When they'd first opened the shop, Duke had written *Customer Service* on the handle in Sharpie.

"I don't know what you're talking about. But you need to go or we're calling the cops." The iron had come back to her own voice, which was good. Snow tried to pretend it mirrored what she felt inside. The sickening urge to jump the counter and sink her jaws into the bald man's pale, plump neck came and went like a flash of heat lightning.

"We are Legion, bitch. And we're not done." The stranger grinned, showing a shiny grillwork of metal teeth.

Beautiful. "Today we are. Get out."

The bald man raised his palms in mock surrender, showing both sizable biceps and an impressive wingspan, and backed slowly towards the door. Snow almost had time to breathe before he feinted back towards the counter in a faux-rush. Duke hoisted the bat back for a shot at the bleachers, and the bald man laughed.

"Be seeing you, bitch."

❋

SHE DIDN'T FINISH HER SHIFT UNTIL NINE. BY THEN THE MOON was already a yellow ball yawning over the horizon, and outside of the cheap plate glass windows that sufficed as the front wall, Snow watched the rain come down, spattering against the asphalt in a black deluge she hoped would wash the last twenty-four hours away.

Her last few appointments had been minor things, trivialities with old acquaintances that her mind could go on autopilot for. Nodding and reminiscing with repeat customers did the trick as her mind wandered, replaying the encounter with the bald man.

Duke, to his credit, didn't ask any follow-up questions. To

be fair, he probably threw someone out of the store with an attitude problem three times a week, so it was possible that he'd interpreted the showdown as some misogynist off the street with an axe to grind. For all she knew, that's what it was.

But how had he known about the spike?

Maybe that was what the LL stood for.

InceLL666.

It sounded crazy to someone who hadn't woken up in a cocoon that morning.

That being said, she'd worn the spike around town at least a hundred times. Crossing the parking lot, playing at the Coma Lounge, the trailer park where her father lived. If the scumbag was local, it wasn't a stretch that he'd seen her. Two inches of silver jutting through the top of one's ear tended to be a bit of an attention-getter. For all she knew, maybe the asshole just had a sick crush.

But she could still remember the sensation, even though she had been bleeding out. The spike between her fingers, plunging into the overripe jelly of the coyote-thing's eye, the hot rush of dark fluid against her palm. The thing keeling over onto the sidewalk, paroxysms racking its frame.

Something had happened then, right before the memory collapsed, caught upon the last frame of the film.

The thing had begun to change.

Percy Blackmore had been her last appointment of the day. He was the bass player for a crust punk death metal act, Dirteater, who sometimes had shared a bill with Bleeding Facelift on midweek nights when business was slow at the Coma Lounge. He only wanted an auricle piercing with a cobalt ring, and as she went about the business, they talked shop for a little bit.

Then he asked if she'd heard about Marquette.

The tears came unwanted, hot and heavy things. Snow

hated herself for them, hated the guilt she couldn't shake. It was like being sick, she realized. The stomach cramped, the body emptied, and the mind was just a passenger left trying to steer through the mess. She couldn't wait to purge it all away.

At the sight of human emotion, Percy threw a hand awkwardly against her shoulder with an arrhythmic patting that unfortunately mirrored his playing style.

Snow straightened, rubbed her eyes with the back of one hand, and gently pushed his arm away.

When they were done, Snow waited until Percy had disappeared before cleaning up her work area and waving goodbye to Duke, who was in the middle of permanently installing a grinning jack-o-lantern on a teenager's calf. Already the hunger pangs had returned, a quake in her abdomen that clutched and shivered, and she wondered if she could wait to eat until she'd made it the whole way home.

The shop was on the outskirts west of town, nestled at the edge of the suburbs that separated the city from the farmland. Behind it was a strand of tall firs that wandered all the way back into the deep hills, a vestigial growth of forest that went all the way back to before Lewis and Clark. In a testament to well-thought-out civic planning, though, there was only one highway that led through it all, and it had a tendency to jam near the tunnel that ran beneath Washington Park. Snow lived on the other side of the Willamette River to the east, and she figured she wouldn't see home within an hour at this time of night.

She didn't know if she could wait that long. The hunger was uncharacteristic, a strange furnace in her gut that demanded stoking. Snow wasn't sure if it was a side effect of her imminent death or if she had just caught a twenty-four-hour bug.

Regardless, she was ravenous.

Steeling herself against the rain as she stepped out into the night, she caught a glimpse of Murder Pie across the parking lot. The aroma of baking cheese and grease hit her, and, just like that, she said goodbye to any sensible dinner plans. Snow started over, sticking close to the strip-mall awning that lined the storefronts.

Maybe that was why she didn't see him.

There was a wet crunch behind her, and when she looked, the bald man from the shop was no more than five steps away from her and closing the distance. There was a black bag in his left hand that looked like a little pillowcase.

Snow yelled, not a scream of fear but to raise the alarm, a warning to any of the dozen patrons nearby that a fellow citizen was about to be done great violence. Her fingers plucked the little knife from her front pocket, another gift from her father.

The sight of it gave him pause. He gazed down at the blade and then her, weighing them both on some internal calculus. If he had a weapon, she couldn't see it.

She yelled for Duke again, hoping that he could hear her over the Type O Negative that he was constantly blaring at window-rattling decibels.

"Put the knife down." The bald man's voice was calm, almost soothing.

"Get the fuck away from me." Snow was steady, but the first chill coursed down her spine, a slight shiver all the way to her fingertips. She had no illusions. He had at least six inches and a hundred pounds on her. If she couldn't run, she was going to get hurt.

"No." The bald man's face grew luminous, pumpkin-white.

A ripple of ill-timed hunger seized her, cramping her abdomen, and it must have read on her face. The bald man stepped in, reaching for the knife, and she slashed it across his fingers in a vicious little arc. He grunted, red lines already dripping from his fist, and Snow yelled for Duke again.

Stop. You're going to need all the breath you can manage.

"Stay." She hissed it at her assailant, trying to circle around him to the Corolla. The asphalt felt slick and wet beneath her sneakers. "The next time it's your balls."

He gave her an affronted look that almost made her laugh. *You're not playing fair.*

"What do you want?" Snow asked, and then another cramp wrenched at her stomach. It sent ripples of ice shuddering through her wiry frame.

It was all the invitation he needed. Before she could straighten up, the big man had already lunged. He was faster than he looked, and though she got the knife up, a beefy palm clamped around her wrist, keeping the little piece of steel from perforating his ribs.

They tumbled awkwardly to the wet sidewalk, the bald man astride her in a parody of lust. When they hit, his two hundred pounds slammed the air out of her lungs, and her head cracked back against the sidewalk so hard her teeth jammed together and bit her tongue. The world went grey and wavered for an instant.

Snow tried to fight, but her dead nerves lost the signal. Even her toes were numb. Raising her head, she spat forged copper.

The bald man yanked her head forward by the hair, then bashed her skull down onto the concrete.

White lights parted and swam before her eyes. Time began to wobble, skipping interstitial scenes like a thrown-together art film.

Snow was being dragged around the side of the building. Wrenched onward by her hair, the burning pain lancing through her scalp did nothing to alleviate the cold surrounding her. The knife had skittered away across the pavement, her bag long gone, both forgotten relics of a better time.

They struggled through the alley behind the shop. One sodden Chuck Taylor came off and flopped on the sidewalk, a breadcrumb leading to her corpse.

Now she was on her side, curled in a puddle next to a red truck. A Confederate flag drooped from its tailgate, an affectation that its owner no doubt thought made him even more patriotic. Despite the agony behind her eyes, all she could think of was her appetite.

The bald man opened the door, and time seemed to snap back into place like a rubber band finally retracted. Her assailant appraised her as the rain fell in her eyes, a weighted gaze she'd noticed ever since she was ten. Leaning over her, he got down on his knees.

What happened then felt like being ripped apart.

The pain in her gut intensified, a shuddering spasm that almost folded her in half. The shock of it was like being submerged in ice, a white numbness so cold it burned. Something inside her shifted as bones began to snap. It was as if she had suddenly become a thing of clay, and a bored preschooler was taking a run at her redesign.

For the first time, she thought she might know what it felt like to explode.

This can't be happening.

It was the only coherent thought Snow could muster over the glacial agony. Organs rearranged themselves into a fine jelly. Flesh ran back and forth like tallow. Her skull elongated, and she found it impossible to make a sound, her jaw collapsing into a sullen, tongueless hole. Great blades of chitin jutted forward from her cheekbones in a rush of blood and grotesque syrupy liquid. Stalks erupted through the thin material of her t-shirt, great skulking lengths of thin black bone as her body bloated and her jeans disintegrated with an audible *pop*, her torso ballooning outward into a dark and spiteful hourglass.

Her skin erupted into fine black hair as her fingers melted away.

She glanced up at her assailant in a mute plea for help, the bald thing that had so recently split her head open on the sidewalk. He was still leaning over her, his grotesque leer now shifting into a comic gasp of surprise, but he hadn't yet managed to back away. Snow was dimly aware through the anguish that her radical redesign had taken mere seconds.

So little time in which to be undone. So little time.

Her vision wavered, in and out of focus. It took her a moment to realize that it was because she'd grown extra eyes.

The bald man stumbled backward to his knees. Her stomach growled.

For the first time in her life, Snow knew what it was to be truly hungry.

Her thin, pointed legs collapsed around him, yanking the bald man down on top of her. They looked like brittle things, but the eight bony limbs trapped him effortlessly. A strange churning began in her abdomen, a frenetic stirring in her gut that wasn't necessarily unpleasant but she had no frame of reference for.

The bald man screamed. The stalks spun him in concerted harmony as if she'd done dance this a million times before. Snow was secreting something, thin and gossamer, that seized upon the man's black boots, and as she pushed more and more of it out of her, it wrapped around his rotating form like an alabaster shroud.

He writhed. He fought. He screamed.

For all the good it did him.

It was over in less than a minute.

Snow rose up, slightly off balance. Her head felt cottony and light, and her thoughts were brittle, unnatural things.

The rain coursed down upon her fuzzy exoskeleton, running rivulets through her tufts of fine black hair.

The white bundle on the asphalt drew her attention. Perhaps it moved.

Snow crouched down effortlessly, which given the sheer number of her limbs should have been impossible to arrange. What passed for her stomach pulsed again, its desire painfully clear. Lowering her head, she sank her fangs beneath the thin cotton.

The entombed form went rigid, then fell still.

Not here.

Gathering the white bundle between two of her many legs, she scurried off, piercing the underbrush and pushing further into the strand of woods that pressed against the strip mall's rear.

When her thirst was slaked, she went off in search of easier prey.

VENEER

The sun cut through her eyelids like a celestial searchlight. Snow did her best not to throw up.

For the first time in days, though, her head felt clear.

Snow forced her eyes open. She was in a patch of yellowing forest, autumnal leaves coating the floor in a fiery canopy. With a groan, she struggled to her feet, feeling the damp earth beneath her, the cool breeze that pushed its way through the old firs. The dawn smelled of forests and wild berries.

And blood. But that was probably her.

In the distance, Snow could make out a chain-link fence, beyond which the improbable track of a small railroad curved along the precipitous hillside below her. The wind struck her bare flesh, a delectable chill that coursed down her spine and tingled her toes. She was almost completely unclothed, the shredded remnants of a black t-shirt now nothing more than rings of torn cotton around her shoulders, but she felt--alive, somehow.

Unassailable.

Reborn.

The night before came in flashes, bizarre and discordant memories that she didn't bother trying to organize but only shuffled back into the deck. Like many late-night revelers the morning after, her first thought was only as to where she might have parked her car.

There was an extra spring in her step as she surveyed her surroundings. It was still early enough that the streets beyond the forest might be empty, and she thought she could find the way she had come the night before, though she wasn't quite sure about that part. Her eyes seemed different this morning.

If she could just make it to the rear of the shop, she'd only have fifty yards or so of sprinting bareass until she reached the Corolla. Her gym bag was in the trunk, and she could throw on some malodorous but passable duds before streaking home to her tiny apartment.

Whatever had happened, whatever *this* was, she could sort it out then.

Aiming for the trail, Snow almost tripped over something half-buried in the leaves. It was a fine white bundle, no bigger than a possum. High-stepping to avoid it, she lost her balance, came down awkwardly, and plunged her leg into a second white cocoon. It crunched bonelessly beneath her bare toes.

She couldn't help but look. Between the torn strands was desiccated fur. Dirt brown specks of arterial blood. A ringed tail.

Snow's gorge rose, and before she could stop herself she vomited, a flood of red gore erupting that spattered the fallen leaves in a scarlet rush.

It's a raccoon, you sick bitch. You've been eating raccoons.

Forcing her stomach back down, Snow wiped the back of her hand across her mouth and straightened up, this time watching her step.

Ignore it. Ignore it all. You just have to make it back to the shop. You just have to--

Something swaying above her drew her attention. Craning her head back, Snow made out a white web, each strand the width of a shoelace, swaying resiliently between two pines.

It was the size of a ship's sail. Little bundles dangled from it like Christmas ornaments.

She thought she recognized a squirrel.

Her mind reeled in a vicious storm. More memories came flooding back of the night before, her expanded frame scampering through the undergrowth, black stalks scaling up bark with nimble grace.

Snow remembered sinking the great scimitars of her fangs into living things. Piercing flesh. Drinking deep.

Snow shook her head. It wasn't helping.

Another gust of wind struck her, coursing over her in a rush of tingling sensations.

Without a word, she hurried back down the trail.

❋

SNOW MADE IT THROUGH MOST OF HER DAY WITHOUT becoming a monster. It made the afternoon something of a win.

After making the successful nude sprint to her car with only a couple of motorists and one very surprised jogger catching sight of her, by some stroke of extreme luck she'd managed to find her bag, kicked beneath the Corolla's front tire in the previous night's skirmish. She'd managed to shrug on another black t-shirt and workout pants in the backseat without anyone being the wiser.

Talbot had been excited to see her when she'd rushed through the apartment's third-floor door, jumping and bounding from side to side as if he'd thought she'd vanished from the earth. It was as if her puppy had drawn up a chair, put the kettle on, and morosely sat up all night worrying about her.

The apartment itself was surprisingly intact, except for the faintest green streaks along the wall below the window. After a moment's examination, Snow let them go.

There was more than enough worry to go around.

She'd showered, fielded a call from her father, wolfed down a footlong grinder at Juliani's that she probably shouldn't have splurged on, and then headed back over to the shop to make her rounds at Duke's. This time, her bag was loaded with snacks.

Forcing her hands to stay busy helped. When they'd pause, her mind would wander in unpleasant directions.

A lot of them included squirrels.

When Snow finally made it home, she'd collapsed onto the small loveseat that did double duty as her guest bed and closed her eyes. Behind her, in the direction of the cramped kitchen, Talbot was munching happily on his brown cereal. Having gone through half of her snack empire, she was only just starting to feel the edges of her hunger creeping in, for which she was profoundly relieved.

In the comfort of her own home, she could have all the kibble her heart desired.

From the lone window, the moon was a swollen chip of bone in a black sky. Part of her wanted to go up on the roof and wallow, counting the stars.

That afternoon, she had come to a couple of conclusions, mulling over the bigger ones while she jabbed new orifices into her adoring public. The first was that the night before clearly hadn't been a dream. Waking up in the woods bareass would do that to you.

The second was that she had, in all likelihood, eaten a

guy. Sure, drank him dry might be a more accurate assessment, but his next of kin probably wasn't going to nitpick it either.

The third, sadly, was that the transformation might not be a one-time thing.

Snow had reached this through a number of unfortunate convolutions. Admittedly, she had never turned into a giant arachnid before, so history was on her side, but she'd never woken up in a cocoon before either. Or had terminal cancer. Or almost been ripped in half by a giant coyote.

Come to think of it, there were a number of new, albeit brutal, experiences she'd stumbled onto in the last seventy-two hours. If her life wouldn't mind settling back down to baseline for a while, she'd welcome the change. The last thing she wanted to do was start spinning webs all over the stairwell.

There was a knock at the door. Snow dropped her eyes to her phone, but there was no green light, no corresponding message. She didn't know anyone besides her father who would just randomly drop by, and so she uneasily tiptoed over to the door and gazed through the peephole.

The knock came again, this time with a muffled cry from the other side.

"Open up, bitch!"

Raven.

Snow glanced back at the kitchen, but Talbot was still munching away contentedly. Opening the door, she hustled Raven inside.

The shorter woman looked like she'd seen better days. Her eyes were a little red, her raccoon mascara a little smudged, and there was a slump to her shoulders that Snow had never seen on the punk fireplug. Even her pink pigtails seemed less than fully animated.

"I'm here checking for signs of life. Shit, girl, you haven't answered any of my messages. I thought something might have happened to you, too." Raven strode into the tiny kitchen, gave Talbot an affectionate rub behind the ears, and grabbed a bottle of iced tea out of Snow's fridge. She threw herself down on the loveseat like she'd been expunged from the heavens. "You skipped fucking rehearsal last night without even a *how-you-doing*. Like, you're playing with my heartstrings here."

Snow's mind raced. In the midst of everything, her phone and social media apps had been the last thing on her mind, with Bleeding Facelift being close to the runner-up. "Shit. Sorry. It's been a crazy week."

"Don't be surprised if Portland's loudest band has to go on without you. Or go on with two bass players. Or four. Or a drummer who plays with human femurs." Raven put her feet up and gave Snow a cool, appraising once-over. "You okay? Fuck, *did* something happen to you?"

Snow's cheeks grew hot, a weight now pressing on her stomach. A stupid sob escaped her throat. Snow hated feeling like this. So many emotions, all skimming just beneath the thinnest scrim. At any moment, one of them might punch through. She couldn't wait until she'd thrown up all the guilt and could go back to being ice.

"I was there."

Snow told Raven about the attack by the coyote-thing, leaving out her own terminal illness, her evening as a giant arachnid, and the fact that she'd hired a hitman online as irrelevant sprinkles on the sundae of her mortality. When she'd finished, Raven loaded that appraising glare.

One of the reasons they'd gotten on so well was that Snow was quiet by nature and Raven's mouth never stopped moving. The unnatural silence between them might be the longest either had ever gone without speaking.

Finally, Raven leaned back and took a swig from the bottle of tea. "What?"

"*What* what?"

"You okay? I say this as a friend." Raven crossed her arms over her Discharge t-shirt. "Marquette got mugged, Samantha. There's no--giant coyote terrorizing Portland."

"Well, not anymore."

Raven just kept going. "And--I'm just throwing this out there--your dog is in the kitchen mowing down on his brown cereal. You're sitting here without a fucking scratch on you."

"I know. It sounds crazy."

"Sounds? Well, yeah. We're all a few cocks short of a henhouse, but come on."

"I can't explain that. But it's what hap--"

The spasm struck her, roiling through her guts like a blast of lightning. The mug of coffee she'd been drinking slipped from her fingers, caroming off the wood floor in a splash of brown. Gagging, Snow tried to straighten up and couldn't.

"Snow?" Raven sat up, concern furrowing her brow.

Trying to scream, trying to warn her, Snow couldn't get out more than a choked wheeze. Somewhere behind her, she heard Talbot start barking, but then the icy fist closed around her entirely. Snow collapsed in a boneless heap to the scarred floor.

The wave of agony eclipsed her.

White fire burst through her nerve endings, radiating an icy numbness all the way down to her extremities. She was aware that her hips were bucking, shoulders shaking, that she was being wracked with convulsions from cranium to metacarpals as some massive weight inside her *shifted*, rearranging muscles and bone into a new whole.

Somewhere in the spreading disincorporation, she felt her organs running together, her skeleton gelatinizing into a pulpy mass. Raven was shouting, but Snow could do nothing to stop it, nothing to halt herself from becoming undone.

In a burst of pain, her eyes retreated as her skull became soft and formless, her forehead flopping over what was left of her vision in a fleshy balloon. Something sick and stretching was happening below her waist, a horrible separation, a rush of elongating hurt, but then her mind altered and her senses shrank. The room disappeared into the dark.

Snow thought that this would be what it felt like to be buried alive.

Then something scooped her up and was moving her, vibrations that she picked up somehow from her legs--

--*tentacles*--

--piercing the air, buoying themselves off her amorphous form. She felt herself lashing out, a rudimentary and unstoppable impulse with the weight of millennia behind it. Then the world became a rush of water, a cool wetness that opened her not-lungs, and she flexed her many tendrils, coursing her body through the rushing liquid and sending ripples of something not unlike pleasure through her vestigial mind.

Something small plopped into the pool next to her, and she sent an investigatory feeler out that way. Whatever it was, it wasn't food and thus held no interest.

Snow was dimly aware that the quivering of the celestial downpour had ceased. Her hunger had faded into a dull constant, and she floated, vapid and peaceful, her tendrils caressing the smooth walls of her pocket sea.

She never wanted it to end.

CHROMATOPHORE

S now startled awake with a gasp in the frigid water, her mouth barely above the rim of the tub. What wasn't already numb felt loose and prune-like.

Raven had nodded off against the far wall of the tiny bathroom, her head curled up against a tattered beige cushion lifted from the loveseat outside. She cracked an eye open, then hopped to her feet. "Hey, bitch. How was your night?"

"What the hell, Raven?" Snow sat up with a splash, her sopping black t-shirt now clinging to her chest. She realized with a start that she was naked from the waist down. "What--"

"That's pretty much how my night's been going as well. Check this shit out." Raven held up her phone and passed it over to Snow. "Towel off. Don't drop that shit."

Snow dried her hands on the hanging cloth and took the phone from her, teeth chattering. There was something wrong with the raccoon punk's arms, but she couldn't quite register what it was over the general shock. Looking past the screen, she saw Talbot at the foot of the tub, wrapped in a little blanket, and panting happily over a bowl of kibble. He was a little damp, but none the worse for wear.

A dull question began to form at the back of her mind as she glanced at the screen. Fearing the light, it wouldn't quite rise to the surface.

At first, she was unsure of what she was seeing.

There was a great blue blob in the middle of her bathtub.

Ignoring her own general pantslessness and Raven's presence, she rose and stepped out of the tub. The water had long ago grown icy, and gooseflesh stood in stark relief upon her skin. Pushing aside any prudish thoughts, she peeled off the wet t-shirt and tossed it into the sink before setting the phone down and grabbing a towel off of the wall. Raven gave her an obligatory wolf-whistle, but it didn't seem like her heart was in it.

Snow dried herself off primly before draping the towel around her chest. "Where are my pants, Raven?"

"Outside. You slid right out of them. Weird shit." Raven took a swig from the apparently bottomless bottle of iced tea. "It's like four in the morning. I've been up all night with you."

"Four?"

"You owe me breakfast, but we'll get to that later. I've been doing a lot of reading." She nodded her head at the resting phone. "You're gonna want to look at that."

Frowning, Snow retrieved the phone. She passed it back to Raven. "The screen locked."

"Even in the future, nothing works." The raccoon punk sighed, pressed a series of buttons, and tossed it back.

As Snow studied the series of photos, swiping her index finger across each, the focus became a little clearer. The great blob wasn't just an amorphous mass of aquamarine flesh, but the central body of what must have been fifteen feet of tentacles, twirling and entangling together like toxic spaghetti.

At the far end of the tub was a small orange anemone, bobbing merrily beneath the water. Roughly the size of a child-sized basketball, it looked somehow content.

She looked down at Talbot. He wagged his tail, darted over, and gave her ankle a friendly lick.

Raven's eyes were locked on her face. For the first time, Snow realized what was wrong with her arms. A series of red raised welts were plainly visible, great stripes of puckered flesh that crossed and intersected like arcane latticework.

A lump began to grow in her throat. "Did I--"

"Yeah. Don't worry about it. I put urine on them to stop your venom." Raven sighed. "Not the grossest thing I've ever done, but peeing on your own arms is definitely a multi-step process."

"Raven," Snow started. Her guilt strangled the rest of the sentiment. "I'm sorry."

"Don't be. Life just got more interesting." Raven waved a seared arm. "To tell you the truth, the stinging wasn't all bad. In a tingly, light shower in the cemetery kind of way. If you've gotten me into BDSM, we'll have to talk later, but right now we have some more pressing fucking concerns. How long has this been going on, Samantha?"

Her real name was a slap across her face. Snow's head cleared, the lump in her throat suddenly gone. "What?"

"Don't fuck with me. Something's been weird with you since before the Halloween party. Right after I told you to go to the doctor, you became all slippery and shit. No pun intended." Raven took a deep breath. "How long have you been a fish person?"

For a moment, Snow could think of nothing to say. "I'm not a fish person."

"Instagram says different."

"This was the first time."

"Mm-hmm." Raven took another appraising sip from her

iced tea. "Like I said, I've been doing some reading online. I'm going to help you, but you've got to be straight with me. Who's the head jellyfish?"

"What?"

"The one who bit you. If we kill him, all the half-jellyfish should return to normal."

Snow tried to wrap her head around this. "Look--"

"Did you make some kind of infernal pact? Do you have a belt made of jellyfish skin? If you do, all we have to do is burn it, and you should be okay--"

"There's no devil pact. Jeez, Rave--"

"Do you have to leave your fish skin behind, hanging from a tree? If I bury it in salt, you should become normal again. Some folklore says all I have to do is say your name three times or scold you, but get real. I've been doing that for years."

"There's no skin--"

"Or you could just start wearing silver a lot and taking vervain. Embrace your full goth. Apparently, that's an herbal remedy for lycanthropy. It might not cure you, and probably tastes like a shit sundae, but it might be able to keep your changes under control. Or meditation--"

"Rave, I--" She stopped and started in her head, finding and discarding half a dozen ways to begin before giving up. "I'm sick."

"Sick?" Raven raised an eyebrow and took another sip of ice tea. "I guess you could call it that, but--"

"No. Like really." Snow exhaled, letting the weirdness of the night try to flow out of her. The air in the bathroom was chilly, the rim of the tub cool beneath her bare legs. "You were right about the headaches. I've got a tumor the size of a golf ball pressing up against my pineal gland that's spreading into the rest of my basal ganglia."

For some reason, it felt good to have it out there. The

look on Raven's face, though, killed any relief. "I've got something like six months, for whatever that's worth."

"Fuck." Raven's jaw hung open like she'd just been kicked in the gut by a horse. Her eyes grew wet and red. "Fuck. Snow, Fuck. How long has--"

"I just found out. Then we got attacked, and Marquette died, and--" Snow searched for the words. "There's more. Last night, I ate raccoons."

"Oh, hey." Raven, for once, looked like she was at a loss for words, then recovered. "Go back to the terminal cancer part for a second. I feel like you're glossing that over with something awesome."

Snow shook her head, not about to tell Raven that she'd paid someone to kill her and then completely chickened out by failing to die. "They're going to run some more tests, but it looks bad. Fatal, actually."

"Are you going to do chemo and shit? Try to fight this thing off?"

"I don't know," she lied. "Honestly, it's taken a backseat to the raccoon eating."

"Coyote." Raven mused. "Jellyfish. Bane of raccoons. Am I missing anything?"

Thinking back for a moment, Snow nodded. "My room. Go look."

Raven looked exhausted as she stumbled to her feet, her pink pigtails bobbing dully. The pair of them walked down the narrow hallway into the bedroom.

The ruins of the cocoons hung from both corners of the ceiling, shredded bags of grey-green fiber like exploded bags of yarn draping almost to the floor. Raven walked over and poked at one with an inquisitive finger. "You've got one hell of a spider problem, Snow."

Snow shivered. The apartment was cold, the heater struggling to survive. She shrugged off her towel and crossed over to the closet to find something warmer. Maybe it was repeated exposure or the long night, but at this point modesty could curl up on the sidewalk and die.

Another wolf whistle burst from the far corner of the room as Snow pulled on a black t-shirt and another pair of jeans. She found an old hoodie and zipped it up across her chest.

Raven was still studying the cocoon, but her eyes were on Snow. "You said this coyote-thing bit you."

"Yeah. Ripped me wide open at the collarbone."

"I've just seen your tits, kid. You don't have a mark on you."

Snow shrugged. "None of this makes sense."

"So, replay. Coyote-thing fucks you up. Then Butterfly Snow. Raccoon-eating Snow. Jellyfish Snow."

"Something like that."

"Fuck. I've got to do some more reading."

SHELL

The basement was freezing, and the folding steel chairs more so. If the group had decided to have the meeting in the back of a sub-arctic meat truck instead of beneath the abandoned Masonic lodge, Snow thought it might have raised the temperature a few degrees.

Marquette's funeral had been the day before. She had been interred in the Merciful Fate Cemetery in west Portland, a rolling green hill parceled out of the deep forest that stretched all the way back to Washington Park. In a true Pacific Northwest sendoff, a fine rain drizzled throughout the ceremony.

Almost a hundred people showed up, many of them from the local scene, punks and metalheads and local musicians in a wave of black. Pachowski and Mgbeke stayed out of the drizzle, standing at a distance from the proceedings beneath a drooping elm, their eyes scanning the mourners like hyenas picking out the juiciest gazelle. When Pachowski caught her looking, he raised his fountain drink in mock salute.

It was a secular affair, tasteful and brief. At the conclusion, Snow had stood at the edge of the great hole carved in the wet earth, casket resting at the bottom. She imagined herself as a great worm, tunneling through the fetid soil, feeling the raw grime rubbing wet against her skin. She would chomp down dirt and think of nothing.

Maybe it would be easier. Maybe she could let herself turn, only never to come back.

A spasm had ripped through her stomach then, the briefest flash of ice.

It was a warning, and she'd scampered away from the pit as if someone had goosed her. Pachowski had yelled something that she couldn't make out across the graveyard, and Snow had given him the finger.

That night she'd sat up with Raven, telling old Marquette stories and eating junk food. At the stroke of ten, she'd turned into a tortoise.

The transformation, this time, had taken maybe thirty seconds, a frozen wave of anguish and reforming that had seemed to last an eternity and left Snow croaking on the floor.

The hunger had returned, but Snow hadn't really been in a position to act on it. When Raven moved too close to her, she'd retreated into her carapace until the raccoon punk had relocated to whatever Snow's reptile brain considered a safe distance, after which she would emerge and chew contentedly on the legs of the coffee table until the whole cycle began anew. Her thoughts were slow and mercurial, and in what felt like minutes but would be four hours down the road, she was herself again.

In the meantime, the raccoon punk had stuck around, doing internet research, playing on her phone, and taking a couple of photos of herself riding the massive reptile. Talbot had become a giant pink gecko, and in every picture, he was snuggling the tortoise.

Snow fished a bag of pretzels out of her bag and began forcing them one at a time into her mouth. Famished over the last several days, her body was constantly screaming for calories, and the urge was becoming almost impossible to conquer. She had become leaner, harder, as if undertaking both a crash diet and draconian workout routine. The transformations had to be burning an incredible amount of energy.

If this carried on, there might not be much left of her.

She got a cup of cheap coffee from the pot brewing in the corner, trying to ignore the flaky crystals floating at the top of it. The room was damp, and a chill emanated from the brick walls that rendered the space almost unusable. In the far corner of the basement, a series of plastic relics from the church group renting the space on weekends had been piled into a jumble of saints and icons.

A dozen people had taken their spots in the ring of folding chairs. Some avoided eye contact, others joked as if this was their local watering hole.

The whiteboard on the easel read simply *Transformations*.

Actually going to the meeting had been Raven's idea. If the weekend church knew what the support group was for, Snow was pretty sure the whole structure would be burned to the ground.

Over the past few days and a bizarre incarnation as a giant sponge, they'd went through a spiral of remedies and cures, curses and invocations. The internet was a never-ending labyrinth of trap doors and dead ends, and Snow had been beginning to give up hope before Raven had stumbled across the bizarre header in one sub-reddit comment thread.

Going through changes? We can help?
Everyone's got questions. We have answers.
Don't be a lone wolf anymore. Be part of a pack.
Transformations.

Taking a seat, Snow gazed at her coffee as if she could read her failure in the dregs.

"First time, huh?"

Snow almost jumped. The speaker was a skinny guy with close-cropped brown hair clinging desperately to his scalp on her left.

He gave her an abashed smile. There were dark circles beneath his eyes. "Sorry. We're all dealing with a lot right now. I didn't mean to pry."

"No, it's okay." The guy was emaciated, all skeletal angles and jutting bones. There was an unusual glow to his fair skin that she thought of almost as a sheen. "Yeah. First time. I don't want to be rude, but I've got to ask. Does this help?"

"Oh, yeah, yeah. I always feel way better after." The skinny guy stuck out his hand. "Dave Pavlov."

She stared at his hand for a moment, grit her teeth, then shook it. "Snow Turner."

"Snow." He mulled it over for a moment. "What are you in for, Snow?"

"Jeez, give it a rest. Am I right?" The man on her other side spoke, a broad-shouldered bald guy with a beard like a rodent's pelt. His red plaid shirt had been rolled up to reveal massive forearms that were folded across his barrel chest. "No one wants to play your twenty questions on their first night."

Pavlov rolled his eyes so hard she thought he might be passing out. "Don't be a dick, Lupe."

"People need peace. This is all I'm saying." The bald guy stuck out a meaty hand. "Snow, yes? Lupe Ig."

Snow gave him her hand, which his meathook promptly tried to crush. She hated contact at the best of times, and Lupe was giving her a harsh reminder of why. When she could retrieve her fingers, she asked the one question she'd had since agreeing to come here. "Is this for real?"

"For sure." Lupe gave her what he must have thought was a fetching grin. "Your name is Snow? Like Snow White? You find your prince yet?"

"Hah." She didn't smile back.

"Play your cards right, I can be your Charming. Dave here can be one of your dwarves. Ha ha." Lupe grinned wider, nothing if not persistent.

Trying to get that ungodly image out of her mind, Snow persisted. "And you guys find this meeting helps? With--with the changes?"

Pavlov nodded. "Afterwards, I feel way more in control."

The clomping sound of shoes descending concrete steps echoed throughout the basement. The room fell silent. A man in a grey suit stepped through the old wooden door, the overhead light gleaming off of his shaved pate. His trimmed black beard was his only conciliation towards ornament. Everything else about him said business.

Trying to avoid Lupe, Snow cast a whisper towards Pavlov, who nodded. "Yeah. He's the doc."

The man in the suit strode across the basement with the air of a patrician, snapping up the last of the folding chairs as if ascending to a throne. When he flipped it around to sit down backward, Snow hated him on the spot.

"Good evening, everyone. Welcome to Transformations." Snow could hear the capital letter. A mumbled chorus of hellos echoed back to him, and the man smiled, exposing too-white teeth. "For those of you that don't know me, I'm Joey Reich."

Another round of greetings bounced around the basement.

"I see a couple of new faces down here." For a moment, Snow thought he looked directly at her, but that was probably just her anxiety. Her concern that she might collapse into a giant meerkat at any moment wasn't helping.

"Okay. For those of you who are new, this is what we're going to do. First, we're going to go around the room and introduce ourselves. Then we'll share our progress this week, and our feelings. Finally, we'll do affirmations. Not everyone has to share, but, of course, we all know how good it feels to get it all out there. Does that sound good to everyone?"

The thought reverberated through her like a chimed bell.

I've made a terrible mistake.

The introductions went around the room, Snow holding her styrofoam coffee cup as a shield while she mumbled her name. Once more she thought she caught Reich surveying her, but then she'd been dealing with wandering eyes ever since she was ten. Snow paid it no mind.

As if on cue, Pavlov hopped up. "Hi. I'm Dave."

Dave. The syllable was an invocation against the empty brick walls.

"As you all know, I'm pretty sure I'm a werewolf. Only my transformation's occurring really slowly." Pavlov held his arms out in front of him like a superhero about to take off. "My index fingers have grown half an inch over the last couple of months. They're almost as long as the middle ones now. Oh, and my arms keep getting hairier. You know, I can't say that I'm looking forward to sprouting claws and howling under the full moon, or all of the carnivorous lunar activities, but right now I'm keeping things under control. I'm just concentrating on being my best self. My human self. Thank you."

"Wait." The syllable escaped Snow's mouth into a vacuum of silence as Pavlov sat back down. *This can't possibly be it.* "I mean, have you ever--"

As one, the ring of metal adopted an indignant expression. The words died in her throat.

Reich coughed. "Snow, you're new to the group, but there are no challenges here. We just let everyone speak."

To Pavlov, he said "That's really great, David. It sounds like you're coming to terms with your transformation very well."

"Thanks, Joey." Pavlov sat down with a thud, his sheen now grown into a full radiance.

Snow surreptitiously eyeballed his hands. He looked as hairy as the next guy.

Were the fingers a little long?

A middle-aged woman lurched to her feet next, her curly hair forming a tight helmet against her bronzed scalp. "Hi. I'm Martha."

Martha.

"I'm a lizard." She took a deep breath, trembled, and let the vibration shake out all the way to the tips of her fingers. "My skin looks normal, but that's how my people fool you. Beneath it is a series of scales. On sunny days I lay out for hours. When it's rainy--and it usually is--"

The group laughed as if on cue.

"--I run my heater at eighty degrees and turn on my humidifier. It's the only way I can heat up my cold, cold blood. You know, sometimes I think about eating you. All of you. As a lizard person, it would be my right to do so. But I won't. I'm concentrating on being my best self. My human self. Thank you."

She sat down. Snow tried to keep her expression frozen to mild interest.

Reich smiled. "Well, we all appreciate you not eating anyone, Martha. It's difficult when you're a dominant species forced to live amongst lesser, cattle-like beings, but you seem to be coping with it rather well."

What did Raven get me into?

It went around this way for a while. People got up, told crazy stories about mutation, self-control, and just a touch of adversity, then sat back down. Reich would give them a verbal cookie and a pat on the head, and then the process would begin again.

She was trapped in a basement with nine crazy people and their enabler. Were there any answers here? Hell, did anyone *actually* change?

"Hi. I'm Lupe."

Lupe. It echoed around the room.

"I'm a Sasquatch. Now, I know what you're thinking. This Sasquatch is not a traditional creature, but we're just as real as the rest of you. Ha ha. One fun fact about us is that we're carnivores. You don't see that very much on the TV. Another is that it's not just our feet that are so big, eh?"

There was a hollow laugh around the room. Even Reich chuckled. Snow was glad she'd given up on men.

"My body's constantly trying to revert back to Squatch mode. Even if I concentrate really hard, and I do, I've still got to shave twice a day. Sometimes I think that I might never find another Sasquatch. Never find true love amongst my own kind. But if that's true, I think I can accept that. I mean, there are all these beautiful human women, am I right?"

Snow was beginning to wonder if Lupe had bodies in his crawlspace.

"So, I'll just mate with you humans, not gnaw marrow from your bones like a storybook giant, and try to go easy on you with my missing link. I'm concentrating on being my best self. My human self. Thank you."

Snow resisted the urge to frantically scoot her chair away as he sat back down.

"Thank you for sharing, Lupe. I'm sure mortal women are the better for your being willing to bone down." Reich gave him a grin and turned his eyes towards Snow. "Snow? Would you--"

"I'm good." If Snow could teleport back to her apartment, she'd leave a vapor trail of glowing dust.

"Are you sure?" Reich's brow furrowed. "I think everyone can attest that the process helps."

There was muttering around her, but Snow shook her head. "I can see that. Everyone's been *so supportive* of each other. I'm just not ready yet."

"Well, all right." There was the slightest note of disappointment, but Reich turned the glow back on like a switch. "Let's all stand for our affirmation, shall we?"

The group rose to their feet as Snow contemplated sinking into the floor. At least they weren't joining hands.

As one, they began their mantra.

"We're all human. At least temporarily. And while we may be bigger, better creatures inside, human is how we'll stay. Ours is not to tear apart our brethren, but treat them with kindness. Friends, not feral. Brotherhood, not bestiality. Consumers, not carnivores. We concentrate on being our best selves. Our human selves."

With that, it was as if a spell had been broken. The group began folding their chairs and catching up over cups of coffee.

Snow bolted for the staircase.

A hand caught her elbow, and she almost removed a number of her pursuer's teeth. But it was only Pavlov, his light sweat now only a faint patina.

He took his hand off her elbow as if it was scalding. "I know what you're thinking."

"I seriously doubt that."

"This wasn't what you were looking for. They don't have the answers you seek." He lowered his voice to a whisper. "But I do. Meet me tomorrow night."

Pavlov must have seen the look in her eyes because he flinched and amended it quickly. "Somewhere public. We'll get a drink. And I'll tell you everything I know."

Part of her did want to wash this entire sorry episode

away in bourbon. With nothing else going for her, what did she have to lose? "The Tell-Tale Bar. Nine."

She even made herself smile as she said it.

DERMA

The Coma Lounge was one city council meeting away from being condemned and one good mosh pit away from collapsing. To Snow, it had become a bit of a second home.

The decrepit building was a mess of masonry in the pit of the Belmont district that looked like it had last seen better days during the Taft administration. The lounge itself took up the first floor and basement of a former millinery which had been subsequently cut up and divided for so many different retail purposes that no two walls were exactly the same. It stood as a miracle of both perseverance and zoning laws.

Going to Marquette's tribute show had been Raven's idea. Snow had initially balked, not just because of the deep-seated guilt she harbored but because it wouldn't get going until nine. Turning into random fauna for most of her recent nights was establishing a pretty mandatory curfew.

Still, Raven had brought her truck, promising that they'd leave at the first hint of any changes and escorting whatever it was Snow became safely back to the apartment. That it might be something with teeth never appeared to cross the raccoon punk's mind.

So it was that Snow slipped the man at the gate five bucks and went inside a door that looked like it had last belonged on a meat locker. Raven was hovering just inside, two black X's adorning the backs of her hands, her pink pigtails bobbing over her studded leather vest. Chains jounced from it in absurd directions as her dark-ringed eyes widened, and without a word she grabbed Snow's hand and pulled her towards the stairs in back.

Snow held up a cautionary finger and stepped over to the bar. Even through the floor the music was loud, vibrating the boards in a sonic fusillade of thumping white noise. Glasses shook dully on the bar, and Snow retrieved a bourbon and soda, ignoring the way the bartender's eyes drifted to the front of her shirt. She hadn't bothered to get dressed up for the occasion, which according to Raven was missing a great opportunity to represent Bleeding Facelift, and the guy was no doubt relieved to see someone who didn't look like they were about to void his security deposit.

"That stuff can kill you." Raven clucked her tongue disapprovingly before she caught herself. "Oh, shit, Snow, fuck me. I'll buy you the next one."

Snow shook her head, forcing Raven to the back and down the stairs. The event was actually kind of sweet. There were pictures of Marquette everywhere, some going all the way back to high school. Her guitar was the centerpiece of a makeshift altar, the top hat hanging off of its head in a jaunty salute. Someone who didn't know might have thought that Clit Commander would have become the next Beatles.

Still, her guilt pressed in on all sides. By the time they reached the foot of the stairs, she was already minus one drink.

As always, though, there was a bar, and Snow took the

opportunity to reload. The stage had been set up in the opposite corner of the basement, and distorted waves of stoned, slow-moving feedback were being belted out as Trinity of Tedium finished their set. Maybe fifty people were downstairs in all, not a crowd but a clustering of black-clad figures moving beneath the red lights, heads bobbing, muted conversations being held with one eye towards the band. There were a couple of standing tables near the back, and Snow pulled up at one of these as Raven procured some kind of toxic energy drink.

Snow scanned the crowd absently, mulling over the meeting. If someone had done this to her, and so sloppily at that, it stood to reason that she couldn't be the last in an unbroken line. There had to be others.

Maybe real weres just didn't do meetings.

Sifting through the crowd of half-familiar faces, she noticed that Phantasm from Hedge's Halloween party was only a couple of tables away, gyrating slowly to the hypnotic thumping as the sludge band wound down. Red hair like a pocket conflagration swung about her strong shoulders, hips swaying in a floor-length black skirt with every dying shriek of guitar.

Snow's eyes lingered for a lot longer than she'd intended them to.

When Raven returned, she'd followed Snow's gaze, clapped Snow on the back, and inquired both as to Phantasm and the weather forecast in the old cemetery. Snow ignored her and gave her a quick debrief about the support group, finishing with Pavlov's offer of more information over drinks the next night.

"Fuck that. You want to know how many times some guy has offered to give me ancient secrets for a shot at the old boneyard?" Raven swigged some of the noxious yellow liquid and slammed it back down. "I'll be your wingbitch on this one. We'll shake him down. Make him regret the day he ever started mercurially changing into a werewolf."

"I don't think beating him senseless is the best option here. And I'll be okay." She remembered how slight Pavlov had looked. "He'd have to put on thirty pounds to be skeletal."

"Was there anyone else like you?" Raven had both elbows on the table and leaned in, kissing-close. "Polymorphs?"

"What?"

"You know. Changing into a bunch of different things."

Snow felt like an idiot. Her own variety had never occurred to her. "No. Everybody just picked another form and ran with it."

"Why the fuck do you think that it is?" Raven leaned in even closer, her mouth inches from Snow's ear. "I've been reading, you know. Folklore. Metaphysics. Morphic fields. Maybe your illness is affecting whatever lycanthropic agent has invaded your bloodstream. Instead of she-wolf or were-snake, you get to roll the dice each and every time."

"It doesn't matter what I become." Snow was surprised to hear herself say it. "I just need it to stop."

Raven grumbled something else, but it was lost in a wave of feedback as the band finished their set by pummeling the music into submission. Snow glanced over at the stage again, but Phantasm was nowhere to be found.

Kind of weird, a total stranger showing up on the night you're supposed to die. Isn't it?

There was a thin pang of remorse and the slightest hint of alarm, but any similar feelings were quickly dispelled when she saw the two men cruising in through the emergency exit.

They were out of place, white t-shirts and drab olive pants in sharp contrast to the black-and-leather clad crowd. One of the men had the barest crewcut, and the other a shaved head and massive handlebar mustache that would have looked amazing on a southern sheriff. There was a militaristic bent to their movement, something a little too crisp in their step and posture.

Anyone could see that they meant trouble.

That she'd almost forgotten that she hired someone to kill her was a true testament as to how bizarre her life was at that moment. Still, Snow forced herself to stay calm. Just because the last bald guy had beat the shit out of her didn't make all of them part of some murder corporation.

Excusing herself, Snow went to get another drink from the bar. This last week had been dreamlike, a sharp fantasy of jagged edges and soft blurs, but at least the bourbon was helping drown out some of her jangling nerves. In her heart, she wondered if the black mass inside her skull had started pressing down on something vital, triggering these madcap hallucinations.

This couldn't be her life.

Someone heavy pressed against her, driving her hips against the counter. Another mass of flesh appeared beside her, propping one elbow up against the hardwood.

"Hey, darling." The mustached man leaned in closer, as if to offer her a secret. He reeked of oil and something darker. "You want to go someplace else?"

Snow tried to push back from the bar, but the larger man wouldn't move.

"What's the hurry?" The mustached man's tone was sedate, almost narcotic. "Can't some old friends talk?"

Snow took a deep breath. She was in a crowded room. Whatever they were going to do, it wasn't going to happen here. Still, she couldn't help but imagine the knife piercing the small of her back, her lungs filling with her own blood. "What do you want?"

"Conversation. I like that." He gave her a once-over through heavy-lidded eyes. "Tim, give the lady some space."

Obliging, the massive Tim took a half a step back. The

larger and angrier of the two, he was probably overcompensating.

The mustached man turned back to Snow. "Do you know how I knew I'd find you here? At this punk bitch's funeral show?"

The errant thought fluttered away before she could grasp it. "No. Why are you looking for me?"

"The same reason there's two cops skulking around upstairs." The words dripped from his mouth. "I believe we have a mutual acquaintance."

"Well, well, well. Look at the fucking bald brothers."

Raven threw herself against the bar and between the two men, pressing up against Snow with a proprietary air. "What, did you guys leave your red suspenders at home?"

"Beat it, bitch. We're talking." The mustached man didn't change expression or tone, only stared down at Snow with flint-dead eyes.

Raven slammed her energy drink down on the counter. "There's no skinheads at the fucking Lounge."

"Raven--"

"Shut it, dyke." Tim spat the words from behind her.

"We're leaving." Snow spat it at him. The air swam with the promise of violence, and Snow was aware of how close things were to spiraling out of control. Head swimming, she reached for a swig of liquid courage and felt a sudden pressure at her elbow, pushing her arm back down.

"Don't drink that." Phantasm was at her shoulder, auburn hair blazing about her face. She was close enough that Snow could feel the warmth of her skin. She nodded up at Tim. "That tall creep put something in it."

Snow held the tumbler up to the dim lights behind the bar. Sure enough, a small white tab was resting at the bottom of the glass, already half-dissolved.

Something in her stomach twisted.

Here we go.

"Hey!" Raven yelled it loud enough to be heard at the back of the room. The band had already cut out to load up their gear, and the words bounced back with almost impossible force against the naked walls of the basement. "Who the fuck do you two think you are?"

The fact that Raven was only a little over five feet tall was an apparent irrelevancy as far as the raccoon punk was concerned. She muscled Snow behind her and put her chin up. All eyes in the Lounge now firmly rested on them.

The room held its breath for a long, drawn-out moment.

Then Raven wrapped a loose chain around her palm and slapped Tim across the face. It made an audible *thwack* that traveled around the room. Snow felt her insides knot as the raccoon punk whirled and did the same to the other man. His mustache did nothing to protect him.

"These two *rapists* are putting shit in people's drinks," Raven announced it to the room at large before she turned back to Tim and Mustache. "Get the fuck out of my club."

The mustached man sighed.

"Bitch--" Tim started, and her hand flew again.

The knot in Snow's stomach tightened. A familiar chill pulsed down her spine.

Oh no.

Not here. It can't be here.

But it was like being violently ill. There was simply no controlling it.

Pushing away from the bar, Snow wormed past Tim and hurtled towards the emergency exit. She saw Raven start to say something else before she caught the look of petrified misery on Snow's face. When Raven tried to follow her, Tim clamped a hand down on her shoulder and growled into her ear. Snow just had time to see Raven knee him in the balls before her hands found the emergency latch.

Then Snow was throwing open the door, racing up the stairs--

A second spasm shook her, immersing her in icy fire.

Concentrate on being your best self. Your human self.

Not a chance.

She plunged through the iron door and into the alley just as the front of her skull collapsed, protruding itself outward into a cone of flesh and gore.

Completely at the mercy of the change now, she skidded hard on the wet asphalt, sliding before tossing her body into a stack of old pallets. Her shirt ripped from her shoulders. Her arms flattened before eagling wider and wider in a series of agonizing pulses. The shoes exploded from her feet in a shower of canvas and rubber. Metacarpals shifted into sickles of bone.

Something tufted from her pores all at once, coating her face, her arms, her hips. It was like being impaled by ten thousand pins that then caught and wavered in a howling gale.

Each new wave brought a rush of nauseating pain. Organs writhed and slithered inside her, rearranging themselves into new constellations of fallen stars. The cone of flesh hardened, protruding from her jaw in a prehensile beak. Her hands simply withered away to bony points.

Snow bucked and twisted in the ruins of the alley until the shocks finally stopped crashing down her spine, mere shuddering seconds that lasted an eternity.

She then hopped to her clawed feet, heart hammering away within her chest.

Snow spread her wings and flew.

HIDE

The cool patter of rain struck her face. Snow opened her eyes.

The sky was grey and placid, the wind howling briskly around her from the east. The wet droplets pelted down against her naked skin, and the shivering sensation that shook through her wasn't entirely unpleasant. Finding her feet, it took her a second to get her bearings, but when she did so Snow let out a sigh of relief.

Snow found herself nestled between the two gardening beds she'd set up on the roof of the apartment building, Mr. Montoya's reluctant concession to her for not repairing her balcony. The plants were hanging on by a thread now, autumn well on its way to having killed them all, but it meant her body had been obscured to all but the most determined oglers from the apartment building across the street.

She was nude, of course. If nothing else, this was making her more comfortable with her own body, but it was murdering her clothing budget. It also meant no keys. No phone.

Getting home wasn't particularly helpful if one couldn't get back inside.

Something clicked from one of the old legends Raven had imparted. Stashing away a set of clothes before one went howling on all fours would probably save you a lot of awkward homecomings. If this was going to be her life--

--please, please no--

--she could at least start planning for it.

At a jog, Snow hurried over to the door obscuring the stairs. By some merciful twist of fate, it had been left unlocked, and as she hurried down the staircase and through the third-floor hallway, she encountered none of her undeserving neighbors.

Hoping against hope, she tried her door. Somehow it, too, was unlocked.

A warning bell went off in the back of her mind. It definitely should have been sealed, but her only alternative to investigating was to die of embarrassment in the hallway. Snow pushed inside.

Talbot gave her a happy bark from the loveseat and rushed over, dancing in circles around her ankles. Snow briefly wondered what he'd spent the night as before she spotted her bag conspicuously resting on the kitchen counter.

A single white sheet of paper had been folded on top of it.

Hey bitch,

Couldn't find you, but you left all your shit outside the Lounge.

I left your door unlocked. Figured you'd claw your way back here bareass.

Hopefully no one took your TV.

--R.

Snow unzipped her bag and rifled through its contents. Everything appeared to be where it should be--

Her phone chirped. Snow glanced over at the clock on the stove. It read 9:46.

Duke's going to kill me.

But there was also a message. She didn't recognize the number, but on impulse Snow clicked on it, a slow roll of anxiety drifting through her stomach.

It was Dr. Pasty's office.

They'd left a voicemail that morning. Snow had listened and then played it back, aware of the hunger already building inside her, not quite daring to believe the words that bounded down the line.

The doctor wasn't sure what was happening. Words like *anomalous* and *unprecedented* were thrown around a dozen times in thirty seconds. The medical team wanted her to come in for more tests, to try and isolate--

She turned the message off, staring at the screen. Snow was so numb she thought she might spend the next several hours as a platypus.

Out of all the jargon, one word had stood out.

Remission.

❋

The rest of her morning had been spent in something of a jittery mess.

Snow hadn't called the doctors back. Not yet. She wasn't sure that she wanted to go through a fusillade of tests and proddings right now. Part of her was scared of what they'd find.

The dark bloom within her--

--*the* second *alien*--

Snow didn't think she was prepared for that kind of scrutiny. They'd brushed the surface of something unusual, maybe even unnatural, and if she wasn't careful Snow could foresee the rest of her life spent in a plastic cage, a lab rat for some government think tank trying to cure aging or build a better biofuel.

She wasn't sure she didn't deserve it.

Of course, if the time bomb in her head went off first--

Her hands were not the steadiest at the shop. Duke cut her off after the first four donuts, reminding her that free food was a courtesy, not a meal plan, and she sloughed her way through piercing a septum, anti-eyebrow, helix, and a wrist dermal with a minimum of small talk.

When she wasn't mulling over the medical report, she was trying to puzzle out who the militant guys at the Lounge had been. Counting her victim, there were three new men who'd stepped into her life as soon as she'd signed on to kill herself. But if they were looking to finish the job, any one of them could have put a bullet in her head the minute she set foot upon the sidewalk. So what did they want?

She'd tried emailing and messaging *inceLL666*, letting him know that the deal was off and that he could just keep the money, but surprisingly the dark web wasn't full of people easy to get a hold of. For all she knew he was in jail, dead, or still just waiting for the opportunity.

Feeling a little guilty, Snow treated Duke to lunch as a *please-don't-fire-me-for-my-constant-tardiness.* She'd been pretty sketchy the last week, and together they plowed through a large triple meat pizza and a bowl of cheesy bread-sticks at Murder Pie.

"Tapeworms." He said it over his large soda, the straw half into his mouth.

"What?"

"You've never eaten more than me. What are you, a buck-thirty? There's a medical phenomenon at work here. I'm guessing tapeworms."

"The wormiest."

The rest of the afternoon was a slow burn. She only managed a bridge piercing and putting steel barbells through a skater kid's nipples, spending the rest of her downtime adding more silver to her ears, listing to droning doom-metal, and arguing the merits of Tieflings over Dwarves in 5th Edition. It was nice to relax for a moment, and Snow had tried to make the most of it, but beneath it all she was worried. If she wasn't piercing, she wasn't getting paid.

The fact that if she took it too easy she might eat Duke was a close second.

PEEL

The Tell-Tale Bar could only exist in Portland.

From the street, it was buried between a paint shop and a vacuum cleaner store that Snow was pretty sure was a mob front. Neither were likely destinations for the bar's clientele, and only the hexagonal coffin dangling from a chain above the black door gave any indication that there was a drinking establishment buried therein.

The interior of the bar had been painted jet black, and ritualistic symbols were inscribed across the walls and ceiling in day-glo neon for a touch of occult ambiance. A framed row of autographed horror icon glamour shots had been plastered across two of the walls, and a small hardwood floor was open in case of any of the patrons felt like swaying to the ambient goth thumping morosely from the speakers.

Snow had shown up early, planning to get a round in before having to deal with Pavlov and what she was ninety percent sure would be sheer lunatic ramblings for the next hour. She'd always liked the gothic trappings of the little pub, but as she plunged into the twilight interior, Snow saw that he'd already beaten her there.

Worse, he'd brought friends.

"Snow White!" Lupe boomed from a booth in the corner. "You, come sit with your favorite dwarves!"

Really?

She almost turned around. Instead she held up a finger, and crossed over to the bar to get a bourbon and soda. Drink in hand, she cast an eye towards the crowded booth. Lupe took up most of one bench, with Pavlov and a small, gloomy man she recognized from the meeting having crammed themselves into the other.

Ignoring Lupe's proprietary pats on the vinyl seat next to him, she pulled up a chair from one of the vacant tables and sat at the booth's head.

Pavlov fixed her with a damp smile. He had two empty gin and tonics in front of him and was settling up with a third. "Hey, Snow. Didn't think you were actually going to show up."

"I wasn't sure you would either. Especially not with company."

"I didn't think that would be a problem. We're all fellow weres here. You remember Lupe and Mercy, right?"

"It is good that you arrived," Lupe boomed. "We have many things to share."

"I've heard about what you're sharing, weresquatch. Not interested."

"Ha ha!" Snow noticed the two empty steins before him, a third half full of some ale with the consistency of liquid bread.

How long have they been here?

Lupe grinned as if they were sharing a secret. "That is good. You are a small thing. The pain would be extraordinary."

She turned back to Pavlov. "Okay. Out with it."

"I watched you at the meeting. You don't think we're for

real." Pavlov tried to hold her gaze but didn't do a very good job of it. "I get it. Some of the people there are just a little disturbed. But it's good that they're trying to talk it out rather than peel off their own skin, you know?"

"At least you're still around." The gloomy man didn't look up from the table.

Pavlov sighed. "Not again."

"People leave the group, drop out of touch." The smaller man's head never moved. "You don't notice it unless you go all the time."

"It's a support group. People flake off. Move around." Pavlov looked annoyed. "Besides, Martha and I have been going for years."

"Martha's one of the reptilian elite. They're probably scared to touch her. And you--"

Mercy paused, trying to choose his words. Snow saw him edging right up to the chasm.

She interjected, both to spare them an awkward confrontation and not wanting to get sidelined with whatever paranoid rant he seemed to be lining up. "To be fair, I might never go back there. Some people just aren't into talking it out."

"Whatever. These are friends, though." Mercy sighed. "It's not the same."

"Don't be sad that people avoid you." Lupe clapped an uncomfortable hand around the smaller man's shoulder. "There are always more weirdos, yes?"

"Anyway, talking it out is the best." Pavlov's eyes were a little wet. "That's why I'm here and not mauling the constabulary."

"So, what's your story?" It occurred to Snow that she knew almost nothing about the trio, and the bourbon was making her a little jagged. She ordered another. "Bad night on the moors?"

"Hardly. My ex-girlfriend's two-year-old bit me." Pavlov sighed. "One minute you're playing with Duplos. The next, you're damned to wander the earth under a full moon."

"What a horrible night to have a curse." Mercy sighed, and the three of them laughed like madmen.

Snow looked away, tried to pretend this wasn't happening. The purple strobing lights swam purple jellyfish across Lupe's skullcap. When he caught her eye, he shot her a filthy grin. She averted her gaze to Mercy, who was a safer bet as he still hadn't looked up.

"You said you knew secrets." Maybe it was a long shot, but Snow thought she might as well try to either reassert some sanity into the conversation or head for the door.

"Secrets might be too strong a word. Maybe rules." Pavlov finished his gin and tonic and popped an ice cube into his mouth. "Conservation of matter is real."

"No shit?"

Pavlov ignored her. "You can't really get much bigger or smaller, only spread your mass out. You're what, a buck thirty? That's all you've got to work with."

"I thought Mercy was a rodent."

"A lemming, but the size of a mastiff." Pavlov patted the smaller man on the shoulder. It was strangely endearing. "Natural laws still apply."

Snow glanced at the other two, who looked as if lycanthropy was the least interesting topic of conversation that could have come their way. "You brought me down here to tell me that the rules of physics are still intact. Thanks for the heads-up."

Mercy nodded over to the bar. "Fascist. Three o'clock."

Some giant with a blonde crewcut had begun shouting from the far stool at someone behind the counter. Uncomfortably, Snow noticed his drab olive pants, the white too-tight t-shirt.

One of them?

The bartender, who somewhat resembled a distant relative of Vincent Price, whispered something under the pounding bass to the raging behemoth. It didn't help. "You know him?"

"Don't have to, sweetheart. It's the ink."

Studying the man a little harder, Snow felt her stomach begin a slow, lazy roll. The trademark lightheadedness that for the last week had prefaced her spending the night on all fours was beginning to creep in.

On his forearm was the black sunburst, an *LL* emblazoned in the center of it.

"What's it mean?" Snow tried to make her voice sound normal, as if the last person wearing that mark hadn't slammed her head into the sidewalk.

"Liberty's Legion. Those alt-right assholes call themselves a political group but just come in from the sticks to stomp people." Mercy smiled for the first time. One of his teeth was missing. "They jumped me last May outside of a cider bar. One of them maced me and the other two set to rearranging my face."

Something about it sounded familiar. "What are they protesting?"

"Human decency."

Snow watched the giant flip over a barstool and storm out. "Nice tantrum."

"There'll be a swastika painted on the wall come morning." Mercy shook his head and took a long sip from the glass in front of him.

"Don't worry, little woman. Lupe is large and powerful. You are safe here." Lupe beamed. It made her skin crawl.

Pavlov drummed his fingers on the table. "Ok. Secrets. Check this out. Imagine that everyone has a morphic field."

"Some imagining." Mercy grumbled.

"Do you get me? Some intrinsic force that makes you take the form of you."

This was going to require more drinks.

Pavlov either didn't notice her glazing over or didn't care. "Something about the lycanthropy throws that field off. Instead of one default setting, your body now has two."

Or ten. Or twelve. Twenty?

"The trick you have to remember is that it's your body. You have mastery over what you are. What your flesh is, and isn't. Even when every fiber of your being is screaming to change, you don't have to let it."

Pavlov held up a hand in front of her. Come to think of it, his fingers did look a little longer. "Eventually I'm going to go full wolf. That's just in the cards for me. But I can put the brakes on it for almost forever."

Lupe rolled his eyes. He'd probably heard the spiel a dozen times. "Or you could embrace the change. Give a big hug to the new you, Dave. Meet plenty of she-wolves."

Pavlov shook his head. "Look at Mercy here."

"Please don't." Mercy said.

"Mercy got tired of following. Now he's his own lemming."

"So there's a way to tell myself no." She wasn't sure why she was trying to make sense of it. "I can control the changes."

"You know your own shape. Better than anyone else. All you have to do is--well, assert it."

Snow paused, weighing her words carefully. "I don't think it's that simple. When my body goes, it goes."

"I bet it does." Lupe offered twenty percent more teeth.

Snow ignored him. "My mind doesn't have a say in it."

"Maybe you're not speaking in a language you understand yet." Pavlov shrugged. "The doc tells it better than I do. You really should give the meetings another chance. Start learning how to talk to you."

"That sounds--" Snow happened to glance down at her drink.

A pale fleck of white, the color of old bone, wafted through the dregs.

Lupe grinned.

❄

THINGS DRIFTED BY IN A MIASMA ABOUT HER.

She didn't think she'd managed to say anything. Hadn't managed to ask for help.

Time started and stopped like a bad projection. They might have talked for hours or just sat there silently. She only remembered that eventually Pavlov and Mercy left. Lupe helped her out to the sidewalk. Then out to his car. Then back to his apartment.

Snow could barely move under her own power, the world a kaleidoscope of threshing parts. Coherent thought felt impossible, and she was jostled up some stairs, over a threshold. Knocked into the center of the room.

She tripped over the coffee table and went down, a bolt of pain lancing up from her knee that she could barely register. Lupe towered above her. Somehow there were three of him.

Then the blast of freezing agony coursed through her, from the base of her skull to her tingling metacarpals.

For once, she welcomed it.

The fog amongst her thoughts turned into glittering crystals and shattered. Her arms scissored outwards as he began to lower himself, serrated triangles of bone bursting through her forearms. Her waist constricted into a narrow stalk with the agonizing crunch of twigs snapping as a separate pair of chitinous legs burst ripped their way from her hips in a puddle of gore. Her pale skin began to harden, soft flesh turning a horrible plastic green.

Things were moving too fast now. She couldn't stop this thing if she wanted to.

Her jaw narrowed into a brittle point with a rush of anguish. Vision blurred as her eyes segmented and, in a moment, there were two dozen Lupes struggling with their belts.

Scissoring feet pressed down on the carpet, knives at the end of her spindly legs.

If he noticed when the mandibles sprang from her cheekbones, he gave no sign.

No indication that her body meant anything.

She was a thing to him.

And he had become a thing to her.

It was nothing for the mantis to lower its jaws.

Nothing to remove his head.

HUSK

She was lying in something sticky.

Dust motes flitted through the filthy sunbeams that forced their way in through the yellow curtains. Snow lifted herself up onto one elbow. She immediately regretted it.

Her head felt like she'd went swimming in a distillery. Everything outside of her raging migraine, though, felt great.

Fantastic, in fact.

But something was wrong. She looked around again. An alarm began ringing at the back of her skull. Snow didn't recognize the place, didn't recognize the drab carpet or the empty pizza boxes moldering on the kitchenette's counter or the beige couch at the far end of the room. Someone had flipped the coffee table over--

--*where am I?*--

--and brief flashes of the night before coursed through her head, a series of shuffled photographs. She'd been drugged once at an off-campus bar when she'd been in junior college and had to have Raven carry her out, who screamed ten minutes of blue-streaked obscenities at the frat boys she'd suspected as the culprits until the bouncer had carried her out too. Snow remembered none of it. Only the second drink, then lights out.

Hard edit. Jump cut to morning.

This migraine felt a lot like that. Pavlov had been speaking. She had thought he was making it up as he went along, and then--

And then what?

Snow made the mistake of looking down.

Her clothes were a shredded mess, but she'd gotten used to that by now. The cemetery was still under lock and key, as Raven would say, and waking up in the altogether had become routine over the last week.

What she hadn't gotten used to was the blood.

It was everywhere, as if there had been a faucet of it that someone had turned on and simply walked away from. Dried gore coated her stomach and breasts. She raised a hand to her lips. A powdery brown crust came away rough on the back of her hand.

She could still taste it. The faintest veneer of copper.

Sitting up a little straighter, she felt it underneath her as well. A puddle of drying scarlet that clung to the backs of her legs. She was resting in someone's blood.

Snow bolted to her feet, feeling the carpet trying to cling to her in gory runnels.

And then she saw it.

There was a mound of human flesh pressed up against the far wall. Its shirt had been torn open.

So had its stomach. A great gaping cavity yawned from below its sternum, an empty bowl of purple-red muscle and bone white.

Its head was nowhere to be seen.

Snow sprinted into the kitchen, one hand clapped over her mouth. Finding the sink, she let her gorge rise and empty in a gout of crimson bile.

Then she heaved again. And again.

Stomach churning, she lifted her head from the mess and turned on the tap, splashing cold water against her face. Slowly, her mind returned. Her thoughts gained focus.

Opening her eyes, she found Lupe watching her. His severed head had been placed next to the sink, the ragged stump of his neck dripping slowly onto the counter and pattering away on the linoleum below. His dead gaze stared into hers from beneath his shelf-like brow, his bald pate speckled with drops of drying blood.

She felt nothing.

Not even revulsion.

❋

Snow sat behind the wheel of the Corolla outside the trailer, idling in the cramped parking lot. Try as she might, she hadn't been able to get the taste of blood out of her mouth.

Talbot whined an inquiry from the passenger seat next to her, and she absentmindedly rubbed behind his ears. Whatever madness he was going through, she hoped he was dealing with it better than her.

She was a monster.

It had taken too long for her to wrap her head around it, but at the end of the day there weren't a lot of other conclusions she could come to. Drinker of blood. Slayer of wildlife.

Murderer.

Snow had stolen a set of oversized clothes from Lupe after doing her best to scrub the obvious gore from her face in the kitchen sink. There hadn't been any bodies in the closet, human trophies, or a bulletin board with red thread connecting random photographs and newspaper articles on the bedroom wall. For all intents and purposes, Lupe had been a normal guy, albeit one who planned to horribly violate her. He had been a mundane monster.

Right until he'd run up against a real one.

Hands shaking, she got out of the car and went around to the trunk, dragging the tote bags of groceries out with Talbot bouncing at her heels. She'd gotten a bottle of bleach out from beneath Lupe's sink and used it on every surface she thought she'd touched, trying to remember anything useful from the hundred crime shows on television and probably failing, but to try was better than nothing.

Another partially devoured corpse. If they found the skinhead in Washington Park, that makes three in a couple of weeks. Mgbeke and Pachowski are going to be ecstatic.

Someone's collecting scalps.

What were her options? If she couldn't control the changes, she was going to kill again. Every time she'd become a predator, she'd made someone the prey. Eventually it would come down to someone she cared about. Even Raven had those long welts up and down her arms, now faded into pink scabs of dry tissue.

She couldn't risk hurting someone she loved.

Which only left her with her two choices.

In movies, the werewolf would move to some remote, national-park adjacent cabin, where they could be a relative hermit and wander the woods at night not hurting anyone. On her salary, Snow could barely afford toast, much less a hermit's hideaway. And while she could pound the bass, screech backup vocals, and paint bloody landscapes, the one thing she was really good at was putting holes in people.

The second option, well--

She'd already tried to outsource it.

Look how well that turned out.

She knocked on the door of the trailer as a courtesy and let herself in. Her father was asleep in the living room nook, slumped over in his chair. A paperback rested on one denim-clad knee. Just like every time she came in and found him like that, her heart seized up in her chest, a pang of regret shooting through her.

He was still the big man she remembered from childhood, giving her piggyback rides and art lessons, nursing her injuries and scolding her more egregious mistakes. The man who'd chaperoned her junior high dances and threatened her high school gym teacher in the parking lot when he'd heard about his wandering eyes. But he was somehow diminished now, as if the sheer force of his personality had gone into hiding. It was strange to be with someone, love them, and miss them all at the same time.

Snow set the groceries down on the counter of the kitchenette, careful not to make a sound, but Talbot had no such compunctions. He raced over to the older man, bounding into his lap.

Lucas Turner startled with a grunt of surprise, noticed his guest, and scratched Talbot effectively on the belly as the little dog flipped onto his back in a gesture of supreme subservience. "Hey, Snow. Thought you had work today."

"I called out." *Duke was less than thrilled.*

Lucas eyed the grocery bags as if they were full of spider eggs. "You didn't have to do that."

"I know." It wasn't entirely true. "You look good."

"I look old." Her father paused for a moment, taking a pull from the oxygen tank behind him. "You know, I was thinking. I love this thing you're doing. You being you."

"I feel a *but* coming on."

"You've got a steady job putting holes in people. I get that. But have you put any thought into your future?"

Six months and counting down. And now I'm eating people.

"Yeah." Snow paused, trying to look like she was reaching for the words. "I've been thinking."

"About what?"

"Librarian." It just popped out. "Limited people. Unlimited shushing. It sounds like paradise."

"Be true to yourself, and you'll never regret it." Her father grinned, then paused, and she could feel him reading her, just as he had a thousand times before, as if she'd broken a plate and was trying to hide it behind her back. "What's wrong?"

There was something so familiar about the question that it brought the last week boiling to the surface. Water collected in her eyes and she hated it.

Her father rose and put an arm around her, the plastic tubing snaking from his nostrils to the tank in the corner. "Hey, darling. It's okay. It's all right."

"It's really not." Snow shook her head, trying to clear away the excess emotion with one sharp swipe. "It's not okay, Dad."

"Do you want to talk about it?"

"I can't. I wouldn't know where to begin, and--" Her hands flew like doomed starlings in front of her face, trying to pluck the correct words from space. "--And, I just can't. Things are spiraling. I feel like I'm losing control."

"That I can't believe." Lucas offered her an abashed smile. "Out of everyone I know, my little girl's the most in control I've ever met."

"Dad--"

"Hush. The fact that you turned out as strong as you are is a testament to you. I wasn't always the greatest dad, kiddo. It's got little to do with me."

A memory drifted behind his eyes. "Remember that time in eighth grade? You had a group project with that Dalton kid and two others. Something about throwing an egg off the roof of the gym, and you had to build something out of drinking straws and hot glue to cushion it."

"Kind of." It was there somewhere, lost in the fog of early adolescence.

"The other three kids just fucked off most of the time, would screw around on their phones or draw dicks or just play video games every time you got together, but you weren't having that. You built this contraption painstakingly, gluing it together straw by straw by straw--" Her father spread his arms wide. "--It looked kind of like a Ferris wheel mated with a beach ball, with this tiny car at the center of the spokes that held the egg. The damn thing took you hours. It was a work of art."

"When the day came to throw it off the gym roof, what happened? Out of everyone's, whose egg not only survived but rolled its merry way out into the parking lot to get creamed by a bus?"

"You work hard. You don't give up. And I love you so much for it. You're the toughest person I know, Samantha. Whatever's going on right now, you'll kick its ass."

FLEECE

The basement of the Masonic lodge had maintained its damp chill, and the metal folding chair beneath her radiated frost like her own personal glacier. Snow cupped her hands around the styrofoam cup of instant coffee and waited.

Maybe it was stupid to have come back here. More than likely, the group didn't have any answers. But at the moment, she needed to be actively trying to fix this. Trying anything.

She watched Martha find her seat next to the whiteboard. Nothing about her shuffle screamed reptilian elite.

Snow's phone buzzed in her hand. She looked down at the screen mistrustfully.

Hey! Rough scene a couple nights ago. You okay?

It was a number she didn't recognize. Before she could decide whether or not to respond or ignore it, another message blurred into existence.

This is Burning Kate. From Coma Lounge?

I was the one who told you those skinheads mickeyed your drink.

A warm flush crept into her cheeks. The redhead.

Phantasm.

She texted to Raven in a flurry of pounding fingers. They threatened to shatter the screen.

Are you giving out my number?

The response only took seconds.

THUNDER.

IN.

THE.

CEMETERY.

Aside it was a blanket scrawl of emojis, kitties and eggplants and an assortment of nonsense. Snow sighed, weighed her options, and was almost on the verge of ignoring both of them when Pavlov sat down next to her.

He looked terrible, which for him was saying something.

She offered him a smile that was only a little forced. Pavlov nodded. "Place is a little dead tonight."

Snow took his meaning. Besides Pavlov and Martha, the only other person there was an elderly man who, if she remembered correctly, was convinced he could become a turtle on the first Tuesday of the month.

"Weird. What happened to Mercy? Or Lupe?" she quickly added. "Where are those guys?"

"I don't know. I haven't heard from them for a couple of days, which is weird. Lupe and I were supposed to go for lunch. You get home okay?"

"Yeah. Yeah." She hoped it sounded convincing. Snow had never been an accomplished liar.

"Good." Pavlov glanced around the room. "Hey, you never mentioned it. What exactly is it you're turning into?"

Before she could fabricate anything, a door opened upstairs. Snow almost sighed her relief. "Here he comes."

The muttering fell silent as Reich descended the stairs, blue suit looking fresh from the dry cleaners. The overhead light gleamed off his shaved pate.

If he was disappointed at the turnout, he showed no sign. Setting his briefcase next to the folding chair that doubled as his throne, he scanned the room with bright blue eyes and offered everyone a sheepish smile. "Looks like we're a little low on bodies tonight. What, has the wolf been at the sheep?"

The other three laughed, so Snow offered a token chuckle.

Try anything, Snow. Try anything.

The meeting went on much like it had the previous night. Pavlov shared that he was slightly more hirsute than before. Martha shared that she'd almost bitten a Girl Scout. Even the old man offered his perspective on proper shell maintenance. At the end, though, Reich turned his eyes to her.

There was no place to hide.

"Snow? Do you have anything you want to share?"

I'm eating people and can't stop.

"No, I'm good."

"The first meeting's a freebie. You don't have to say anything. But after that, you've got to buy in, Snow. Buy into the idea that we can all help each other. That we can all control our changes."

"I've got anxiety."

"Don't worry. We're all friends." He spread his arms wide. "The first step towards healing oneself is admitting that you're hurt. Whatever you say doesn't leave this room."

"Basement."

"Basement, then."

Snow sighed. "Do you always gang up on the newcomer?"

"Let's try this. Maybe you can just answer a few questions instead." He smiled. "How long has this been going on for?"

There was something interrogatory beneath his tone that she didn't like. "Couple weeks."

"And what is it you feel like you're turning into?"

A serial killer. "Plenty. I'd rather not elaborate."

Reich paused, folding his hands in front of him for effect. "Mm-hm. And was there any particularly stressful event a few weeks ago? Something that may have instigated these feelings?"

"Yeah." He was good at what he did, just leaving these poignant silences at her doorstep that she felt obligated to fill. "I had a friend who died. Who was murdered. I guess you could say it's been a tough time ever since."

"And you were there."

"Yeah." She sighed, a long exhalation of guilt. "And I couldn't stop it. Or stop them. It's been fucked up ever since."

"Trauma can be an awful thing. What you have to remember, Snow, is that it might feel like it's your fault, like you did something to put all of this into motion, but everything has a higher purpose. Everything happens for a reason."

Snow almost laughed. "You've got the first part right."

"Your friend wouldn't have wanted you to feel this way. You've got to take control again. It's the only way you're going to be able to get through this." Reich gave a brief glance to the other participants. "Are you sure you don't want to talk about what it is you're turning into? Your particular transformation? We might be able to help."

Something about him grated against her. Snow had the peculiar sense that she was missing something, something just beneath the surface, but was so relieved at the obvious chance to exit stage left that she let it go.

"No. No, you've been great, but no."

✳

THINKING ABOUT PHANTASM'S TEXT, SNOW CONCOCTED, THEN discarded, half a dozen appropriately witty responses. She had almost driven back to the apartment and settled on the best one when the change blew through her.

The wave of ice struck her all at once, a death rattle from the base of her skull to the tips of her toes. Panicked, she gripped the wheel of the Corolla even tighter and whipped her head from side to side, searching for a place to dump the car beneath the streetlights and cursing Portland's general parking congestion after nine pm.

The mantra played back to her, as ridiculous as she'd thought it was.

Concentrate on being your best self. Your human self.

She didn't know if she believed it, but it was her body. Her will. She was in control. And she wouldn't--

The pain was intense, almost blinding. Her torso began to swell and stretch beneath her black t-shirt, and with a last gasp she whipped the Corolla against an empty curb, tore the keys from the ignition, and poured herself out onto the street. She recognized North Belmont and the empty field beyond. Was it a park? A cemetery? It didn't matter now.

She just had to get off the street.

Snow stumbled across the asphalt, agony staggering her steps, and threw herself into the hedges.

The leap was the last thing she could control. Apocalyptic spasms wracked her nervous system, sending her bucking and writhing against the grass as her feet melted away, shoes left as empty and alone as gutted shells. Pressing together, her legs rippled and merged, flesh and bone fusing in a gelatinous agony from her waist down as her skin expanded to accommodate the pair. Snow felt her hands retreat into her arms, and then her arms into her torso, meat pooling and reshaping at the whim of some celestial molder as her torso continued to lengthen, stretching and stretching away like a piece of clay rolled by a child.

Her skin became coarse, then hardened. She opened her mouth to scream, and two scimitars erupted from her upper jaw, shredding her lips in a gory eruption. Snow's eyes narrowed to slits, her nose now nothing more than two dark holes as the change wrought its work.

The first thing she felt was a virulent hunger, but she was quickly bested by the autumn chill. Something was wrong with her body, sinking from cold to freezing, and Snow slithered further into the park in search of shelter. She was immense now, a fifteen-foot rope of muscle all guided with a singular purpose, weaving farther and farther in amongst the standing stones.

She knew where she was, if only dimly. Clouded images came to her of the pioneer cemetery, the graves of Portland's founders, the immense crypts they'd left in their wake. All drifted by devoid of context, a heap of meaningless dreams. Snow pushed herself harder against the ground, willing herself to move faster. The chills wracked her, and she was running out of energy as quickly as if someone had opened her veins.

Prey would have to wait.

An unmoving shadow rose above her, blacking out the streetlights, and Snow crawled closer. Pressing her ropy bulk against the structure's bricks, she found a gap in the masonry. Struggling harder, she forced herself through the hole. The jagged edges of the gap drug bloody furrows in her scales, but she was beyond caring as she plowed her way into the darkness of the crypt.

There was safety inside. There could be warmth.

It was a chore to squeeze even the very tip of her tail through the ragged opening, but in the end she'd made it through. Snow nestled before the entrance and prepared to fall dormant, counting on her own mass of slithering coils to keep her warm.

Something small scuttled in the darkness. A scent hit her wide nostrils, and a dry rattle exploded from her tail.

She wouldn't have to go hungry tonight after all.

SCALE

Beams of light filtered in through the dirty rectangle above her. Snow knew them as the first weak rays of dawn.

She felt the chill of concrete beneath her skin and struggled to her feet, the last six hours a blur of images and sensations she'd rather not examine at the moment. That she could remember anything at all was progress of the darkest sort, and what that might preface she chose not to consider. At least, not until she'd had some coffee and enough breakfast to sink a barge.

Her hand flicked up to her ear. The rings were gone, and the holes that bore them were as closed and smooth as a baby's skin.

I'm somehow healing. Every time I change, the odometer resets to zero.

A dry, sweet musk hit her nostrils, the scent of antiquity and aged rot. She placed a hand on the cold stone wall and tried to get her bearings. She was nude. Again. And unless she'd let her gothic side lapse her into full Countess Bathory, this wasn't her apartment.

She'd been in North Belmont when her body had decided to rebel--

Oh no.

They'd visited the Lone Fir cemetery when they were younger. The old pioneer cemetery was a staple of the town, a baroque lot that housed some of the founders and their ill-fated brethren, and the tall mausoleums and verdant grass were always visible from the road. Raven and Snow had been given to taking long strolls there at dusk during a younger, more goth phase.

Snow willed herself not to touch anything. Already her mind was turning over what the deep shadows at the far end of the chamber might contain.

A bitter chill seeped from every corner of the tomb. Pressing herself against the rectangle of light, Snow felt rough wood itch beneath her fingers. She searched for a knob, a latch, anything, but there was nothing there.

Why would there be?

A pang of hunger, and then white lights danced in front of her eyes. Her breath quickened. Snow was famished, but more than that the first real panic was beginning to dig in. She pushed at the door, then really put her weight into it and heaved. Nothing.

Thankful that she couldn't see what else was in the crypt with her, Snow shoved harder. The door settled on its frame, but that was it.

Snow took a deep, coarse breath. Conscious that she'd just filled her lungs with the dry miasma of rot, she spaced the tomb out in her head. The hinges were clearly silhou-etted by the morning light, so in theory the lock would be--

She took a step back, drove a leg up, and kicked at the spot. Then harder the next time. The door barely moved, and each blow was like driving her heel into a brick. The idea that a quick transformation might actually help did not escape her, but with her luck she'd probably turn into a flying squirrel and spend the next six hours just cleaning herself.

Snow took another few steps back, her bare buttock scraping against something cool and smooth as the grave. Suppressing a shiver, she ran at the door and pistoned her foot into where she imagined the lock should be.

I'll show you thunder in the fucking cemetery.

Two things happened. Something in her foot tore at the impact, a twinge of agony that rattled up her spine, but the latch also snapped, wet wood ripping loudly from the frame in an outward shower of splinters as the door shuddered open. Snow almost cried with relief.

If there were any groundskeepers nearby, they would be grabbing for their shotguns.

The early light was blinding after the crepuscular darkness, and Snow staggered out of the mausoleum with a hand over her eyes, her feet finding purchase on the wet grass. Her body was covered in grave dust, her right foot aching and raw, but at least she was finally free.

Snow shambled onto the main path, half-dragging her leg behind her. She knew full well that any onlooker treated to the sight of a nude shambling woman in a graveyard should aim for the head first and ask questions later, but she would just have to take her chances.

Always a little modest, Snow was surprised what half a dozen walks of shame had done for her confidence.

She found the thoroughfare that led by the south end of the cemetery and hurried towards it at a high limp. The morning was overcast, the first hints of rain blowing on the light breeze, and Snow was surprised at the sensation against her skin, how right everything felt despite the ache in her right leg, how pure and clean it was to have your bare feet in the grass, naked muscle working beneath an empty sky--

A muffled gasp came from the row of stones to her left. An elderly woman was on her knees, a bouquet of flowers leaning against a granite marker beside them. Her jaw was agape, and she was making the sign of the cross with the frenetic abandon of a world semaphore champion.

Snow blew her a kiss as she shambled by.

Then she was at the road. Lingering in the foliage, she scanned both sides of the causeway without success and hoped that the car hadn't been towed. For one nauseating second, she thought it may have been, but then she spotted the Corolla to the east.

Limping down the sidewalk, she reached the car and thrust a hand under the back bumper. A pickup truck drove by, slowed, and almost stopped, but when she saw the red of its brake lights she bared her teeth. Whoever was behind the wheel thought better of their dalliance and hit the gas, roaring off into the distance.

She pulled the emergency key out of the magnetic container and popped the trunk. The bag was where she'd left it, no small favor, and she threw open the door to the backseat and tugged on another t-shirt and a pair of gym shorts she'd have to burn as soon as she got back to the apartment.

The thought that she was getting better at this was not a consolation.

✳

Snow had just finished getting ready when Raven forced her way through the apartment door.

She barged in towards the bathroom like the world's smallest bull in its tiniest china shop. "Hey, bitch! Are! You! Ready! To! Stumble!"

Snow inwardly groaned. Calling in Raven for support

might not have been the best tactical decision, but she knew that, left to her own devices, she would just chicken out and skulk in the apartment, painting morose doom-laden scenes while doing a middling wallow.

Burning Kate, *nee* Phantasm, had texted her while she was carving up new victims at Inktropolis. It had stayed light, just a little flighty, a little flirty, but Burning Kate had wound the stream of characters and emojis around to an art walk that night in the Alberta district. She had a space she was co-opting with a number of other local artists and would be showing off some of her wares. There would be snacks and box wine, if maybe Snow wanted to stop by?

The thought filled her with physical dread. Worse, a certain longing she hadn't thought of in a long time.

True, it wasn't a date, and possibly the very worst way to meet someone was to gaze over their artistic offerings and choke up platitudes. What if it all pointed to some dark, unavoidable flaw?

It didn't matter if she didn't like it. Snow was a firm believer that there was no bad art, only things she didn't connect with. With seven billion people crawling the planet, the trick was just finding the right audience. She'd worked hard enough to know how difficult it was to finish something, and harder still to put it on display.

Still, she wanted to connect with Kate. If Phantasm had some weird duck fetish, obnoxious deviance, or obsession with rubber hoses, maybe it was better to kill the whole affair at the outset.

Maybe it was a little irresponsible to go out knowing that she could change, and Snow had initially demurred the outing on account of being a monster, but Raven had twisted her elbow, promising she'd butterfly-net her at the first sign of trouble and pitch her into the back of the Corolla. She still wasn't sure that she shouldn't be chained up in the basement of the apartment building until she figured out how to control the changes, but she let herself be talked into it.

Talbot, ever vigilant, greeted Raven by hopping around her in excited semi-circles that may have had more to do with the paper bag full of Chinese food cartons she was carrying than the raccoon punk's positive attitude.

"Bitch! Eat something and let's go!" Raven leaned on the doorframe, pink pigtails bobbing in the yellow light. "Hey, shit! You done gone and got pretty!"

"Shut up." It was hard to hide her smile.

"Thunder! Cemetery! Thunder! Cemetery!" Raven slipped around behind her and began dry humping her hip. "If I was into girls, you wouldn't stand a chance."

Snow pried her off. "Thanks, but do you remember the last one of these we went to?"

"Not in the slightest. Nice rings." Raven flicked at her ear. "Is it just me, or are your piercings moving around?"

Snow sighed. She'd spent the better part of her lunch wolfing down a massive sandwich and putting new holes in her ears. It hurt a little, but after the mind-altering agony of the last couple of weeks, they were less than paper cuts. "Every time I change, they fall out. When I come back, even the holes are gone, so. New holes."

Raven twirled one pigtail between her fingers, taking a second to process this. "So you also have super healing."

"No. Yes. Maybe." Snow took a deep breath. It was now or never. "I need you to do something for me."

"Nigh anything."

"I mean, I'd do it, but I don't think I can make myself, if that makes sense."

"Nope. Start talking."

Snow went to the kitchen and rummaged through a drawer, producing the heavy carving knife. "I want you to cut off my finger."

❋

THE WIND HOWLED AROUND THEM ON THE NARROW CITY street, a fat and yellow moon waning away to nothing above them as they huddled together. The east wind was acting up at the worst possible time, and the EZ-ups and displays lining the sidewalk had to be held down with gallons of concrete or free weights to keep them from whipping away into the night like grotesque kites.

Nonetheless, there was a healthy crowd of people trying to remain earthbound as they milled about and perused whatever wares the local art community had to offer. Snow was a little surprised by their persistence, but the city was about to collapse into the grey morass of winter. It was the last chance to walk outside without three layers of clothing for the next five months, and more than a few of the citizenry were taking it.

As they passed the next booth, a middle-aged woman was desperately clutching at her watercolors, trying to prevent them from taking flight.

Raven whistled. "Great fucking party!"

Snow wasn't discouraged. Sure, the three blocks they'd passed so far had looked just about ready for FEMA relief, but Kate had said that her co-op was in a brownstone tucked neatly off of the main boulevard. As long as the masonry didn't blow over, Snow would still get a chance to feel this out.

Talbot, however, was in distinct danger of becoming airborne. She scooped him up under one arm, his leash now dangling against her side, and she felt the warm flick of his tongue against her inner arm.

The three of them strolled past an elderly man selling wooden chessboards, and Snow spotted the flimsy street sign rattling in the breeze. "Turn here!" she cried back to Raven.

Raven nodded, her eyes watering in the gusting wind and threatening to turn her raccoon mascara into black metal corpsepaint. "You realize I love you, right? Why are you doing this to me?"

"Sorry." The side street was even more dimly lit than the main thoroughfare. Alberta was one of the oldest neighborhoods in Portland, and some of the narrow streets still had steel rings embedded in the sidewalk to hitch one's horses too. The infrastructure had yet to catch up with the next century, and what few light posts could be seen burned a dull and hazy orange.

Snow counted street numbers as they walked, trying not to think of what she'd say, how she could manage to not trip all over herself. At least the rundown buildings on either side of them were providing some shelter from the budding hurricane.

Raven surprisingly had declined to remove her finger, citing her plea as self-sabotage. Snow's romantic drive-by would be awkward enough without her dripping bloody gore all over the warehouse, and while a red-swathed hand might be a great conversation starter, most questions would have to center around her sanity.

After they'd gotten home, though, it was on. Snow had bartered and cajoled until finally Raven had signed off on taking the last knuckle of her little finger.

She found herself fidgeting the pinkie against her palm, wondering how badly it would hurt. Would it really would grow back, or was this was a sign of her completely losing it?

I have to know, right?

I am in control of my own body. Not some coyote. Not some cancer.

Concentrate on being your best self. Your human self.

Finally she spotted the building. The co-op was in what looked to be an old auto garage turned into a small warehouse, with one massive track door wrested all the way up to the ceiling. Light spilled out of the opening like a dying star, and she could hear music and the low susurrus of conversation pouring from within.

A hand clamped over her shoulder, and Raven spun her around. "Hold on," she tutted, giving Snow a once over and brushing flippantly at her dark hair. "Ok. You look good. Remember, kid. You do you."

Snow nodded, her voice now vanished. With a swallow, they went inside together.

Whatever she'd expected, this wasn't it.

Harsh mechanical sculptures filled the warehouse from floor to ceiling, great arcing constructs of welded scrap metal and spare parts that looked precariously poised to topple and crush any onlookers foolish enough to wander too close. Once past the initial gauntlet of figures the floor opened up a little into a few tables, some folding chairs, and a hastily constructed dance floor in one corner beneath spinning colored lights. The latter was adjacent to a welding area and what looked to be a small foundry in the far corner, where behemoths lurked beneath great canvas tarps as if waiting for their chance at resurrection.

Maybe a dozen people were walking around, studying the sculptures, and talking amongst themselves. Snow, not proud, went straight for the box wine.

Raven rolled her eyes but said nothing. Snow sipped from her plastic cup and scanned the crowd. She didn't spot Kate, and instead turned her attention to a beetle-mouthed anthropoid with a wide torso constructed from perforated metal. Its claws were extended stars from its basketball-sized palms, and either a carapace or cape drooped low over its trunk legs.

"Looks like a Transformer fucked a bug." Raven appraised.

Snow sighed. She'd known what she was getting into.

Talbot whined appreciatively and tried to sneak his tongue into her cup as they moved on to another sculpture. A spiral of jagged iron and spare parts had been welded to a steel cable that snaked upward to a massive hook on the ceiling.

"Knife Tornado."

A steel pole stretched from a welded base, a series of irregular chrome wings sprouting from it at odd intervals.

"Flutter Dick."

"That's not a bad name for it."

Snow turned around, the butterflies in her stomach taking flight.

Phantasm snaked an arm through hers and tapped their plastic cups together. "Cheers!"

For a moment, Snow's words escaped her, the only feeling being the warm corded muscle of the other woman's arm against hers. Kate's auburn hair had been tied back, revealing sharp cheekbones with the faintest smudge of soot beneath one of them. She was wearing a Misfits t-shirt and a flowing umber skirt over black boots, and Snow found herself struggling to focus.

Raven flew in off the top rope. "Woman of the hour! Which one of these Mecha-Godzilla's is yours?"

Kate looped a thumb back over her shoulder. "Knife Tornado. I saw you come in, but I figured you should have a chance to get comfortable."

Snow felt Raven scoop the puppy out of her grasp as Kate withdrew her arm. Not used to the contact, it felt even stranger now departed. "This is some set-up you've got here."

"You like it?"

"I was expecting a little more granola and hackysack."

Smile, Snow. Normal people smile.

"We're not that kind of collective. I play with fire." She

emphasized the last by banging their plastic cups together. Snow sipped from hers and found it almost empty.

"Come on, I'll get you a refill."

Snow followed the other woman back out into the collective, conscious of the sway of her hips, the hard muscles in her shoulders. The light, warm feeling grew and spread in the pit of her stomach. She tried to ignore it, and in doing so allowed paranoia a shot at ruining her night.

The thoughts came unbidden, one after the other.

She'd never seen Kate before hiring someone to kill her, and the redhead had pursued her, not the other way around. This meet-up had been her idea, and even now she was being separated from her friend and loyal companion.

Snow had always imagined *inceLL666* was a man, but what was that based on?

Kate filled her glass to the brim with an anonymous red liquid that was almost certainly full of cyanide. "So what is it you do? You don't exactly strike me as a nine-to-fiver."

"I put holes in people." *I also become a different monster every other night and consume the rogue citizenry.* "Do a bit of painting. Play bass. I'm thinking of going to library college. All books. No people."

The last she hadn't told anyone, not even Raven. It had seemed a moot point after the terminal illness and cyber hitman, but now that one was in remission and the other had either fucked off with her money or was now making small talk, maybe the future was looking a little brighter. If she could just stop eating people, the world might be hers.

She glanced suspiciously down at her drink, but there was nothing out of the ordinary floating in it.

"That's really cool. That you're looking to the future." Kate gave her a smile, and Snow was surprised by the warmth in it, the general empathy burning in her emerald eyes. "I don't know what I'm going to do when I get tired of all this."

"Your stuff is really good. You shouldn't let yourself get discouraged."

"You're sweet, but my stuff is lethal. There's a limited client base who are willing to put razor wire in their own homes." Kate bit her lip, then moved on. "This is going to sound really forward from someone you've only met a couple times and only once on purpose. Do you want to go do something? Like this weekend?"

Snow felt a rush of heat to her cheeks, aware that her pale skin was probably turning fire engine red. If this was an assassination attempt, maybe she'd really been missing out.

The world swam for a moment in a blanket of warm cotton, and she heard herself rather than spoke the words. "Yeah. That'd be cool."

"Great! What do you--" A faint line creased Kate's forehead. All warmth and charm evaporated when she looked past Snow's shoulder. "Hey! You guys aren't welcome in here!"

Frowning, Snow turned around.

The night exploded.

❊

SHE DIDN'T FEEL THE IMPACT. TIME JUST SKIPPED A COUPLE OF frames forward, until Snow was only aware of a wash of white stars swimming around her and the feel of cool concrete pressed against her flesh.

Kate was shouting something, and a harsh male voice was growling smugly back at her. Snow lifted her head and saw a number of legs approaching from both sides in a vertiginous tilt of the axis.

A chill shivered from the base of her spine to the nape of her neck, and Snow quavered.

Whatever else happened, she could not do that here.

Would not do that here.

Groggy, she pushed up to her hands and knees, not quite able to take the extra step of getting to her feet while the world still seesawed around her. Her skull rang, a sick knot of pain uncoiling under her right eye, and she was able to put two and two together pretty fast.

He sucker-punched me. That fuck sucker-punched me.

She heard boots against concrete running over. Raven, with a stream of profanity issuing from her mouth that Snow could only process in a series of corrupted warbles. Shaking her head, she tried to clear the fog away.

The mustached man from the Lounge looked down at her.

"Hey, bitch," he grinned. "We were just talking about you."

"Stay down," Kate warned.

"This doesn't concern any of you," Mustache might have been just asking for directions. There were twelve inches of lead pipe dangling loosely from his right fist. It took Snow a long time to put it together.

Is that what he hit me with?

A crowd was gathering, maybe half a dozen artists in coveralls or torn jeans behind Kate. Another three men with too much testosterone and free time glowered behind Mustache. Snow thought she recognized Tim's crewcut.

"The cops are on their way. Get the fuck out of our place." Kate spat. This didn't sound necessarily true, but Mustache appeared undeterred in any case.

"Let them. You're a bunch of socialist hippies in an art commune. The cops don't care." Mustache shrugged.

"Good," Raven barked, waving two feet of metal that looked like a collection of thorny vines. She'd tucked Talbot protectively away under one arm. "I'll fuck you with this sculpture until your dick works like a sprinkler."

Snow staggered to her feet, ignoring Kate's hiss to stay

down. Before she could take a step forward, Tim stepped in behind her and looped an elbow around her chest. It was like being clamped in chains.

"We're just going to have a word with your friend here," Mustache smiled. "It's been a long time coming. I'm sure she agrees."

From under Raven's free arm, Talbot made a noise. It wasn't his normal whine, or an excited bark, or his frustrated growl. A sound she had never heard before was pouring out of his throat.

"Shut that dog up." Tim's voice was surprisingly high, almost lilting.

"Fuck the dog. Let's go." Mustache waved a hand, and Snow felt herself being lifted off her feet, tugged backward.

She heard Talbot howl, then shriek. It pierced the air and eardrums with equal impunity, freezing the room for one fractured moment.

With one hard kick, Snow drove her boot down into the big man's instep, just the way her father had taught her. She thought she heard something snap as Tim groaned, and the chain loosened. Without thinking, Snow threw her elbow into his solar plexus.

He doubled over, but there was no time to get away. Mustache was already swinging the pipe at her, the Legion rushing forward on both sides.

Everything happened all at once.

Raven screamed. Not yelled or swore but actually screamed, a sound Snow had never heard before and hoped never to hear again. Six feet of whirling grey muscle leaped from her grasp, a rope of scales that was all mouth and writhing flesh. With perfect clarity she could see its naked jaw yawning open as it traveled through the air, rings of concentric yellow teeth jagging outwards in hundreds of needle-thin points.

It struck Mustache just above his left cheekbone and latched on with one savage bite, closing down over the socket of his eye.

Tim sputtered. "They're throwing fish!"

Mustache howled as he wrapped two beefy palms around the giant lamprey and tried to pull it free. Blood and something yellowish, thicker, dripped from around its jaws and spattered his brow.

The ropes of muscle started to fatten, the coils of its body growing thicker.

Talbot, or at least the terrier, was nowhere to be seen.

At a loss, the two Legionnaires behind Tim just stood there, torn between having to touch the slimy hide of a giant eel or cracking heads or simply taking off before the cops got there. Whatever they'd signed up for, this was above their mental pay grade.

Snow had taken a step back towards the art commune, mercifully free, when she felt the first shiver caress her spine. A thin bolt of ice slithered from her brain stem all the way down to her toes.

"Raven!" She didn't mean to scream it.

The raccoon punk was at her side in a heartbeat, throwing her head under Snow's arm and whipsawing her towards the door.

Something flopped behind them in a series of wet slaps against the concrete. Snow glanced back to see that the lamprey had detached itself and was now beginning to struggle after them.

A dozen mouths hung agape. No one wanted to get near it, and it was a small wonder. When Snow caught a glimpse of the mustached man's ruined face, she saw why.

He now wore a mask of blood, dozens of weeping wounds lacerating his scalp, his cheekbones, his nose. Where his left eye had been was now a gory red ruin, and he clasped a hand over the missing orb, a series of muffled shrieks coming from his torn lips.

The whole room smelled of hot iron and fresh blood. Snow limped back a few paces and took the lamprey in her arms. Coiling around her neck affectionately, it gave her a playful squeeze.

"Ugh." Raven offered, yanking her towards the door. Another pulse of ice quickened in her veins, sending tendrils of numbness out to her fingertips, and then they were outside in the blustery night air.

The lamprey licked her cheek with a warm, bloody tongue.

MOUTON

Raven had just managed to hurl her into the backseat of the Corolla before Snow lost all control. They spent the next four hours driving around the thinning city streets, Snow aware of a burning hunger for something she'd never tasted. Every now and again the stranger in the front seat would roll the window down and she could force her snout out into the cool night air, a temporary reprieve from the suffocating reek of oil and plastic.

She only got to do it a couple of times, though.

They were getting some pretty weird looks.

Eventually, her appetite took over. She tried gnawing on the back of the seat, but the mix of foam and vinyl were barely edible. With no recourse or food on hand, Snow curled into a furry ball against the grey-scaled fish monster and went to sleep.

✳

THE RAP OF HARD KNUCKLES AGAINST THE WINDOW WOKE HER. Snow cracked an eye open.

She was sprawled out on the Corolla's back seat, the yellow glare of a streetlight casting weird shadows through the glass. Her shirt was stretched to all hell but still intact, which was a minor miracle. With one sweeping hand, she found her jeans scattered somewhere on the floor. Snow rolled herself onto her back and yanked them on awkwardly over her hips. Talbot looked back from the passenger seat, his little pink tongue panting in apparent rapture.

For once, her clothes weren't a complete waste. Maybe this was starting to look up.

Raven stood on the curb, her pink pigtails bobbing sagely in the wind. "Hey, bitch."

She sounded tired, and Snow realized that the sky had grown lighter. How late was it? "What time is it?"

"Three-something. You sure know how to show a girl a good time."

Snow gauged her surroundings for a moment and recognized that they were on the street outside the apartment. Juliani's Deli was just a couple of storefronts away. "Thanks, Raven. I really appreciate it."

"Don't thank me. How many times do I get to chauffeur a giant guinea pig and a snake monster around town?" Raven held up her phone. Sure enough, there was a massive rodent snuggled into a ball in the Corolla's back seat, a grey and hideous lamprey draped across it for warmth. "I'm going to send it in to one of those weird-animal-friends websites. Kind of heartwarming, in a make-you-barf sort of way."

Snow got out of the car and stepped onto the curb, her human legs only giving her the slightest inkling of discomfort. "No. I mean thank you. If it wasn't for you, I'd be running bareass around the Alberta District right now. And who knows where Talbot--"

"That was awesome." Raven grinned. "One minute I'm

holding a dog, then I've got a weaponized fish. Hope that Nazi asshole likes his makeover."

The raccoon punk ran her fingers beneath Snow's eye and bit her lip. "Sweet Johnny Ramone. There's not a mark on you."

Snow nodded. She didn't even feel a bruise. "Was it bad?"

"He caved half your face in, kid. Bones were broken." Raven whistled. "You still want to lose that finger?"

Snow shook her head. Memories were discordant, floating by at a breakneck pace, but she seized on the one that she thought really mattered. "Kate. Was Kate okay?"

"You mean Phantasm? Yeah. Or at least she was when we bailed out the door. Figure since they were after you, they didn't give two shits about the local steelworker's union." The raccoon punk gave her a grin that would make a long-shoreman blush. "Thunder?"

"Cemetery." Snow sighed but felt herself smiling, which was ridiculous. Even after a brawl, a fish monster, and knowing that she couldn't stay human for more than a minute if the mood took her, she'd met someone, albeit someone who may be trying to kill her.

They were going out that weekend.

Play it cool, Snow.

Raven touched two fingers to her brow in a mock salute, then changed her mind and hugged Snow fiercely. "Fuck. Be careful, weirdo. Watch out for those guys."

"I will."

"Assholes like that, they don't give up. Whatever those fascist fuckwads want you for, we need to figure that shit out." Raven detached, gave her a wink, and began the eight-block walk back to her apartment. She called over her shoulder. "Any of that Chinese food's yours now. You took a couple bites out of your backseat, so I'm sure you're probably starving."

Snow scooped Talbot up out of the Corolla and strolled to the apartment building's entrance, fumbling for her key. She felt refreshed, as if she'd just taken a quick vacation to another world. The wind felt sweeter, the moonlight somehow fuller. As she unlocked the door and hurried up the two flights of stairs, she started thinking about Kate.

Don't get your hopes up.

Keep your expectations low.

Waiting for her to murder you is probably a good start.

Still, it was so weird to be trying again. After everything that had happened in the last few weeks, everything that was still happening, who would have thought that this, of all things, could be the result?

Unlocking her apartment door, she hurried inside and let Talbot go. Paws skittering on the carpet, he rushed over to his bowl of brown cereal and began noisily chomping away.

Snow eyed the Chinese food on the counter, weighing whether or not to bother heating it up. Her hunger was a yawning crevasse in her stomach, and she plucked a bowl from the counter, threw some rice, noodles, and kung pao together. In great sticky spoonfuls, she began to demolish it.

In under five minutes, she was scraping the chopsticks against the ceramic sides of the bowl and searching for errant rice. Realizing its futility, she was going for a second helping when the spasm shook her, a bolt of ice that might have fallen from the sky.

Her fingers went numb, the bowl clattering to the linoleum floor. Talbot had a moment to look at her before darting behind the loveseat, his contented rumbles suddenly contorted shrieks.

Twice in one day.

Twice in one night.

Time stretched out in an elastic band. She was boneless, collapsing, a rough sack of meat thrown on the carpet.

Something hard and ridged thrust upward from her back, shredding through her black t-shirt in an eruption of gore as her arms retreated, legs dissolving in a pool of flesh and blood to coalesce into a sopping yellow-green mess. Writhing in anguish, her eyes fell out of her head, and she was aware from her new vantage point that the bony mass protruding from her back was swelling outward, ever outwards in size.

Between the waves of agony, she saw it knock over a chair, pushing the little table over to one side.

She raised her eyes, aware that they hadn't been lost at all but were somehow still connected by fibrous stalks of muscle. From high above the carpet she saw the biggest cockroach she'd ever seen stumble out from behind the loveseat, a black and glistening thing that rubbed at its thorax and seemed to be having a lot of difficulty getting around on six legs.

The sight of it sent her retreating into her shell.

❄

WHEN DAYLIGHT CAME AND SHE WAS STILL A SNAIL, SNOW knew she was in trouble.

Time had slunk by with astonishing speed. The day moved as if someone had taken the sun and tossed it across the sky. She'd slimed her way across the kitchen floor for a couple of passes if only for the sheer novelty of it, but it was futile.

What was there in the apartment for her to eat?

Instead, Snow watched Talbot scuttle around on his new legs and noisily finish off the three cartons of Chinese food that had been left on the counter, no doubt fulfilling the dreams of every insect since the Cretaceous period. Her thoughts were slow-moving waves that took forever to reach shore, but she found her increasing awareness a confusing burden.

In the beginning, it had been so much easier when the animal-self had taken over. But somehow her mind was remaining more and more, even if she had as little power in this form to alter her environment as the couch did.

Talbot seemed to be having a pretty grand time of it, though, wandering around and rubbing against her swollen shell with a contented chittering that set her thousands of teeth on edge. For her part, she simply oozed back and forth across the linoleum and tried not to do anything that would invalidate her deposit.

The sun was a high ball of fire in the sky by the time she retreated back into her shell.

She dreamt.

It was afternoon when she woke, a naked woman in a light coating of mucin. Try as she might, she couldn't bring herself to call Duke until she'd showered and mopped the floors.

He was as thrilled as she thought he'd be. She weathered the epithets and veiled threats as best she could while scouring the cabinets for food, wolfing down bowls of stale breakfast cereal and trying to not taste them. The day was a lost cause, and Duke wasn't up for her only coming in for a couple hours before the shop closed.

He wasn't mean about it. That wouldn't have been in his teddy-bear nature. But in the kindest possible terms, he advised her to get her act together before he'd have to put another piercer in the shop.

The smell of the deli below her wafted in through the open window, but she tried to ignore its siren song. She was already out a day's wages plus tips, and with the late appearances, no-shows, and the way the past couple of weeks had been going, rent and helping out her dad might be on their way to diametrical opposition. She wasn't quite at the ramen three-times-a-day meal plan, but neither was avocado toast suddenly on the menu.

She sent out a brief text to Raven, letting her know that it had happened again. Raven replied almost instantly.

There was another message on the phone from her doctors about running more tests, staying on top of this remission, and warning her of the potential for relapse.

She had to seriously think it over.

Half your face was caved in. Bones were broken.

Just because the black mass pressing against her cortex was in remission didn't mean it would stay that way. Even if her body rejected her piercings and knit itself back together after every change, who knew what effect that might have on a tumor? For all she knew it changed shape with her, and every animal incarnation she'd been thrust into had carried the same time bomb in their skulls.

For all she knew, the remission was a totally separate event from her near death.

Coincidence. No such creature.

She'd put out a hit on herself, and something had tried to kill her. Was it that simple?

That it wasn't some wiseguy with a sniper rifle was hardly a surprise. You couldn't get a decent used car for two grand, so it's not like the best of the best would have been lining up to put her out of her misery. A redhead with a penchant for fire, for example, might have decided to branch out into the business.

Or someone with the change had decided to monetize it.

She remembered slamming the spike through the coyote-thing's eye, the hot rush of blood and ichor that had poured over her hand. The way it had seemed to shift the moment she lost consciousness.

Snow was almost positive it was dead. But what if it wasn't?

What if there was more than one?

Who else could the Legion be? What else could they want with her but to finish the job?

She picked up her phone again, intent on relaying the revelation to Raven, when the icy burst flashed through her from head to toe. A wave of agony so intense as to wrap all the way back around and border on pleasure coursed through her, dropping her to her knees.

The phone clattered to the floor, her hand now losing the shape to hold it.

No.

Stay human.

It's your body. Yours.

But it refused her.

✳

IF RAVEN HAD COME IN FIVE MINUTES EARLIER, SNOW MIGHT have bitten her face off.

Snow had spent most of the afternoon and an early portion of the evening as a one-hundred-and-thirty pound alligator, which had provided a couple of side benefits but had left Talbot, who'd become a small yellow duck, hiding safely on the kitchen counter for most of their cohabitation. Ill-suited to apartment life and the cold besides, Snow had once more found herself unable to eat anything of merit and only waddled around the confines of the small apartment looking for a place to settle in and ambush easier prey.

Her thoughts were weighted objects, dragged down by the pervasive chill and a need to conserve her energy at all costs. Her metabolism had slowed itself down to an almost stasis, but her keen nostrils when she settled in to lurk were fixed on the door. She wasn't sure why, but something told her dinner was coming,

Coming soon.

She'd awoken in a dark apartment, her t-shirt stretched to hell and her bottoms nowhere to be found. Talbot was licking her face with wet happy kisses, no doubt eager to share the floor again and more than a little traumatized. She rubbed him behind the ears groggily and got to her feet.

White stars danced in front of her eyes, and she put a hand on the little table to steady herself as the apartment lilted around her. The pang in her stomach howled with indignity, and she shoveled a handful of stale cereal from the open box on the table into her mouth as she poured out a bowl of kibble for Talbot.

The terrier crunched away as if she hadn't fed him in days.

The door opened behind her and the lights flickered on.

A loud wolf whistle pierced the apartment.

"Bitch, I didn't know it was that kind of party!"

Snow looked down at her bare hips, the t-shirt covering nothing, and shrugged. Mooning Raven was barely an indignity at this point. "Shut the door before my neighbors start snapping photos."

"What's that smell?" Raven asked. Snow didn't know what she was talking about. The aroma of melted cheese and red sauce that the raccoon punk had brought in with her made her stomach growl. "Crack a window, snowflake. It's like a fucking reptile house in here."

"I spent most of the day as an alligator." Snow popped a window open and noticed her jeans protruding from halfway under the couch. She tugged them on without the faintest immodesty.

This is your body. You're in control of it.

You're in control of it.

"No shit? Again?" Raven set the box down on the table and ripped it open. The hot scent of fresh pizza engulfed Snow. "Figured you could use a snack. Nothing to eat around here but the furniture."

"Which I tried. You're a lifesaver, Raven."

"And you're my favorite naked friend. What the fuck, Snow?" Raven threw her a paper plate, and Snow tore off a slice. Without thinking, she devoured it in eight noisy bites. "Why all the shifting? What's changed?"

"I don't know." Almost burning her fingers, Snow ripped off another slice. "Maybe this is how it's supposed to work. Maybe eventually I'll just settle as something else and never come back. Just stop being me."

"For starters, there's no *supposed to*." Raven pulled out a chair and sat, pressing both elbows against the table. "The world's a wobbling ball of chaos hurtling through the cosmos at sixty thousand miles an hour. There's only what you can and can't do."

"I can't stay human right now." Snow felt a heaviness in her gut that had nothing to do with the food, a warmth rising behind her eyes, and she tried to force her emotions down. "I can't keep doing this."

"Shit. There's got to be a way to control it. Otherwise, the news would be full of were-this and were-that." Raven put a hand over hers. "You know what I think it is?"

"Lycanthropy?"

"That's only for wolves. No, changing all the time." Raven took a bite of her pizza, popped the top off a can of some vile energy drink, and washed the whole mess down. She waved the slice around like she was conducting an orchestra. "You've got someone in your life. Scratch that, someone you're interested in. You've spent so long frozen solid that now, when you're finally thawing out, your anxiety is kicking into overtime. You're afraid of losing control. And so you do."

Snow nodded, a little unsure. "This sounds new-age."

"Meh." Raven took another sip. "I've been reading up on it. There are all sorts of temporary fixes, wolfsbane and belgrave and dead man's hand--"

"Yes, please." Snow started. "Let's try those."

"--But, ultimately, everything's going to revolve around you. This thing, you see it as an intruder. A parasite. Something *other*. But what you've got to come to terms with is that there's no getting rid of it. This thing is you."

"There's no cure." Snow felt her stomach drop, even as she went after another slice. At least the bad news was being balanced by the influx of calories. For the first time in days, her appetite was starting to wane.

"None that doesn't end with me burying you, no. And my shovel budget looks like shit." The raccoon punk looked somber, almost thoughtful. "This is now your default setting. The sooner you come to grips with that, the better. It can't be caged, but it can be controlled. We're just going to have to figure out how."

"You said you'd been reading? Reading what?"

"Old occult books. Self-help guides. Reddit." Raven shrugged. "I've got the next couple of days off. I can drive you to work, get your groceries, shove food in your mouth when you're human. Promise not to eat me and you've got a date."

Snow opened her mouth to respond, but then the glacier crashed through her spine. From her upper lip, two massive incisors erupted, lengthening into foot-long tusks with a wrench of nerve-shattering pain.

"Gross! Okay! This is it!" Raven shouted, pushing herself back from the table. Her voice had gone high and nervous. "Relax. Focus on you, Snow. Concentrate on being your human self. Your best self. You can feed the beast later!"

Snow kicked over her chair, crashing to the floor on all fours in a paroxysm of pain. Her torso swelled, her jaw expanding as her arms melted back into her shoulders in an agonizing rush, leaving the barest flaps of bony skin in their place.

"Relax! Focus on holding your form!" Raven yelled from the far corner of the room. "Make a deal with the monster!"

Snow tried to rise above the suffering, to find a handle with which the torment could be steered, but there was simply nothing for her to grasp. As her jeans audibly shredded, legs merging into one massive muscular stalk, she felt her organs shifting, bones melting and rearranging in waves of icy agony. She tried to concentrate with all her will, trying to strike a bargain with the change.

"Ease up! Ease up!" Raven was edging slightly towards the door. "Fuck, think happy thoughts!"

Nothing happened.

Snow howled through her reshaped mouth at her tissues reknitting, her hard muscle suppurating into flab. A coarse brown fur thrust its way through her pores, and she writhed against the carpet as Raven tried alternately to cheerlead and cower.

Finally, the shock ebbed and the waves of agony retreated.

Snow found herself pleasantly warm.

A small penguin wandered out from behind the couch, tottering uncertainly on its two little legs. Without hesitating, it waddled over and pressed its little beak to her cheek.

Breathing hard, Raven snapped a picture with her phone. "Well, at least there's that. You two are fucking adorable."

❄

SHE'D WALLOWED AROUND IN HER NEW FORM FOR MOST OF THE night, occasionally bellowing as Talbot awkwardly sprinted about and crashed into chairs. At something of a loss, Raven kept a couch between her and Snow, tried to coach her out of it, and then gave up and spent the next several hours hurriedly scanning through web content before finally passing out.

The problem was that nothing Raven uttered sunk in. She could hear the sounds, feel the emotions behind them like colors on the spectrum, but whatever filter she needed to run them through for comprehension had been misplaced. After flopping about at the raccoon punk's commands, Snow had tried to insinuate that the coaching wasn't working.

As a walrus is not the master of nuance, this was harder to get across than it would seem.

Shortly before dawn, Snow changed back. She found herself once more naked, freezing, and the recipient of warm doggie kisses on her kitchen floor. Not bothering to dress, she just went for the cold pizza.

Raven startled awake from the chair. For a moment, it appeared that she had no idea where she was, and then her eyes found Snow. "Hey, bitch. I've got to say, if there's an upside to this, werewolfery appears to be making you hot as shit."

Snow gobbled down a slice of pepperoni in four bites. "Yeah. I feel sexy as hell."

For the first time in days, they laughed. None of it made any sense, caught in the absurd gears of a chaos engine. All Snow could do was stay on top of it and try not to get ground into paste.

Tired of annihilating her wardrobe, Snow fetched her lone robe out of the bedroom, taking a moment to look at her paintings as she did so. Surreal, doomed landscapes. Blurs of color and streaks of raged frustration. When was the last time she'd tried to create something? When did she last find time for this?

When she found her way back to the cramped living

room, Raven was resting her feet up on the tiny coffee table. "So, you can't hear me when you're changed?"

"Can't understand you." Snow went straight to the pizza, which had become dangerously depleted. "Something doesn't click over all the way."

"Okay." Raven drummed her fingers on the arm of the chair, her pink pigtails bobbing in the dim light. "From everything I've read, admittedly a lot of it fictional, you've got to focus on staying you. This is your body. You're the one in charge."

"Concentrate on being my best self. My human self." Snow said it without a trace of irony.

"That's the ticket." Raven mused. "Find a place in your brain, and, like, check-in with yourself every couple of minutes. Not just when you're going to go all rubbery."

"It's my body."

"Correct."

Snow breathed. For a moment, she felt in complete control.

Then she thought of the Legionnaires. Of warm, inviting Kate. The dark bloom that might still be rooted in her skull. That someone out there might still be trying to kill her, who very well might be the aforementioned Kate. Her father in the future, living on the street without her.

She was ramping herself up on purpose, trying to see if she could pile on the added stress and stay herself. She wrapped her humanity up in one iron hand and clenched onto it, willing herself to not let go.

Inhale.

Center herself.

A couple of minutes later, her grip slipped.

✳

THEY TRIED FOR THE NEXT COUPLE OF DAYS TO SLOW THE shifting down.

During her brief stopovers in humanity, Snow was aware that her life was slowly rotting away around her. She hadn't been to work for days, hadn't even been able to operate a phone to call out. Raven had been on the line with Duke one of the times she'd stopped over as a person, making excuses for her and inventing some grand illness. Maybe it would tide him over and maybe it wouldn't, but the bottom line was that without that cash flow there were going to be real problems. She was already stretched thin, paying the rent on two places and supplementing her father's pension.

It was bad enough being evicted from your own body. If she couldn't straighten this out, both of them would be out on the asphalt before too long.

Despair was starting to weigh her down, concrete boots dragging her to the bottom of a well. Maybe that hitman hadn't been the worst idea she'd come up with.

Raven had tried coaching her up during Snow's meager stints as a meatbag, for whatever that was worth. In the meantime, she'd enjoyed runs as a meerkat, a porcupine, a salamander, and as a giant ant. For the last, Raven had politely excused herself with a promise to check back in later. Apparently her guru powers would not extend to a hundred pounds of clacking mandibles and skittering chitin that kept trying to carry her back to a nonexistent nest.

When human, Snow began to shape her thoughts. Maybe Raven had been onto something.

She remembered the coldness that flowed through her when she was piercing. Inhaling, then centering herself, right before she ran them through. In that moment, everything was relative, and hers was the power to shape flesh at will. If she could hold onto that razor-thin glacier, everything would remain in place. She could stay herself, control her morphic field, all that shit. If she could just hold on.

The problem was that she couldn't.

Snow snapped awake. Cold and floating, she felt like she was back at the beginning.

For the first time, this was somehow reassuring.

She was floating in the tepid waters of the tub, nude as par the course. Raven dozed idly by, lounging against the doorframe of the tiny bathroom. A dozen or more red rings lined her arms, forming abstract zeros against the healing pink welts.

Every time Snow came back, she was healed and better than ever. Only the people around her bore any sign of the consequences.

If Snow were to pick up the raccoon punk's phone, she was sure she would see her latest transformation, Talbot as no doubt something cute and vaguely associated. It didn't matter now.

This body was hers. She would hold onto it.

As quietly as she could, Snow fished a hanging towel from off the rack, dried herself off, and stepped nimbly over Raven's snoring form. She ambled towards the bedroom, aware of the pain in her stomach, and pulled a black DHD t-shirt out of the pile. Tugging it on, she realized how strong she felt. Every drop of excess had been boiled away over the last few weeks in the forge of transformation. What was left was pure, undiluted *her*.

A blank canvas stood in front of Snow.

She found her brushes and began to paint.

EXOSKELETON

"So, nothing?"

"Nothing."

Raven had come in a couple of hours later, marveling at first at Snow's bare ass but then at the work in progress. A whorl of deep verdant greens and black and blue bruises, the blasted nightscape was starting to come together, a portal into another, albeit more abyssal, world. "Where are your pants?"

"I'm down to two pairs of jeans. I didn't want to get paint all over them."

They'd gone downstairs to Juliani's for lunch. It was a remarkably clear day for autumnal Portland, and they spent it at a wrought-iron table out on the sidewalk. Snow ordered a sandwich roughly the size of her head.

"You seem--different." Raven offered.

"I feel different." Snow smiled. "All that work you put in. I think I'm finally able to put the pieces together."

And it was true. When she felt herself slipping, she could find that needle of coldness. Inhale, center herself, then run it through. Having discovered a handle, she was gripping it for all she was worth.

In the meantime, what good was worrying about it? About any of it?

"I called her back." Snow couldn't keep the excitement out of her voice. "We're going out tonight."

"Do you think that's safe?" The raccoon punk tried a poor attempt at nonchalance. "I mean, this *was* you last night."

She slid her phone across the table, and Snow peered at it. What looked to be about ten feet of blue squid was bobbing merrily in her tiny bathroom tub, a happy pink cuttlefish circling around it.

"I'm sure. I think I've got this."

When their food came, Snow tried to relax. She ate with determination but not speed, trying to savor the individual flavors as they came across her palate: the vinegar dressing, the ripe tomatoes, the quasi-bitterness of the cheese, the savory bites of meat. Taking her time, she kept one hand on the ice below.

She was in control.

Snow just had to make sure she stayed that way.

※

STORM CLOUDS WERE GATHERING AROUND THE CEMETERY.

Snow had picked up Burning Kate in her slightly chewed-up Corolla, planning on downplaying the bite marks in the upholstery. The topic never came up.

She'd dressed up a little bit, which meant no band shirts and only the barest consideration to makeup. When she'd seen Kate, she had been glad she'd made the effort.

Phantasm looked amazing, her hair cascading around her shoulders like a miniature conflagration. She wore a blood-red skirt over scuffed black boots and a simple black top, which showed off rather than hid the hard muscle of her shoulders. The latticework of tiny burns that dotted her forearms was on full display.

Snow felt a rumble down in the pit of her stomach. For once, it had nothing to do with hunger.

They went out to a movie at the old Hollywood Theater, a two-screen holdover that mixed in small new releases with art films and blasts from the past and served pizza and beer alongside the popcorn. Snow, never the biggest cinephile, had let Kate pick the entertainment. Kate gleefully pointed them to John Carpenter's *They Live.*

At the concession stand, Snow caught Kate glancing sideways at her. For no particular reason, she wondered if she were studying her prey.

How does one inquire as to whether or not their date is planning to murder them? "What's up?"

"Just looking. Your face--" Kate tried, then shrugged. "I thought he got you pretty good, but look at you. There's not a mark on you."

"Trick of the light, I guess." Snow made a show of studying the concession board. "Besides, I'm a fast healer."

"Don't think we can say the same for that guy with the mustache." Kate whistled. "My eyes were on the fight. Where the hell did that eel-snake thing come from?"

"I don't know, but I'm glad it did." Snow kept her grip firmly on the lever, not wanting to begin their date with a pack of lies but also not with tales of shapeshifting and madness. "Did they start anything after we took off?"

"No, they just grabbed their guy and left. Cops never did show up, come to think of it."

"Ugh."

"Here." Kate held out her phone, and Snow looked into it, half-wondering if this was a distraction and the knife was about to slide between her ribs. The photo was of a galvanized steel lamprey spiraling downward, a stick figure skull between its jaws. "Kamala's calling it *Snakes of Wrath.*"

"Whoa." It was remarkably lifelike, right down to the little collar around its neck.

They reached the front of the line, and Kate slipped an arm around her waist. "You a cider girl? Portland Cider's local, and it's pretty incredible."

"Whatever works in a pinch."

"Four ciders," Kate called to the man behind the counter. When Snow raised an eyebrow, Kate gave her a wicked grin. "Trust me. You're going to need more than one."

A drink in each hand, they wandered into the dark theatre. Picking out a spot near the back, they sipped at their drinks, a delicious nervous energy growing between the two of them that Snow felt intoxicating. When the lights dimmed, Kate slipped her hand into Snow's. The warmth of her skin against Snow's ice was unusually comforting, endearing without being over the top. Snow drank a little faster than maybe she ought to have and tried not to put too much thought into it.

Never having seen the movie, Snow didn't know what to expect other than eighties madness. An hour and a half later of aliens, sunglasses, and professional wrestling, she was not disappointed.

Credits rolling and synth music blaring behind them, the two of them spilled out onto the street together, fingers interlaced, laughing and a little buzzed from the cider. For a moment, Snow was worried that this might be the end of the night, and a pang of anxiety rattled down her spine.

"You're not done yet, right?" Kate gestured across the street towards a sign reading Sam's Billiards. "Do you want to get a drink with me?"

Snow smiled, inhaling slowly. Centering herself.

After ordering drinks at the bar, the pair of them found a

corner booth nestled far in the back. Every accidental contact, every brush of a shoulder, was awash in sensation, and Snow's mind was buzzing with newly rediscovered feelings. It was ridiculous, she knew, but also glorious. At some point, she was sure to burst.

But she was relishing a night free of forms and shifting, She was finally behind the wheel of her own body, one hand firmly clamping the changes into place. For the first time in weeks, she felt like herself.

Better, even.

"I'm just going to come right out with it." Snow took a deep breath and cracked her neck. *Here goes.* "Are you an internet hitman?"

"Huh." To her credit, Kate didn't bat an eye. "Would I tell you if I were?"

"Valid point. Would you?"

Kate made a show of mulling it over, her auburn hair blazing above her shoulders. "Yes. Yes, I think I would. Because I wouldn't want to start this--us--by lying to you, and I could always deny it all later."

At the mention of *us*, Snow felt a flood of warmth flow through her, but she tried to play it cool. *Stay human, weirdo.* "So?"

"I am not, as you put it, an internet hitman. How about you? Did you just call me out here to talk shop? Because you're going to be pretty disappointed."

"I am not, nor have I ever been, a contract killer. So this isn't an elaborate ploy to end my life?" Snow knew she might be weirding Kate out, but the tension had been building for so long that it was coming out in a rush.

"Do most of your dates start out this way?" Kate smiled. "No, I'm not, nor was I ever, planning your untimely demise. Those assholes who showed up at the commune, though. That might be a different story."

They drank and talked more, minor stuff to start off with, then slightly deeper. Kate was the fourth of eight children, an escapee from the quiver who, outside of an older, equally escaped brother, had little to no contact with the rest of the family. She had a bachelor's in art history and a welding certification that the little burns on her arms called into question but that she chalked up to enthusiasm. As for how she'd intersected their little group, Kate had met Hedge at a Coma Lounge battle of the bands four months ago. She'd thought he had been a little sweet on her until she realized he was gay, but had finally found someone to talk seventies rock with and had ended up going to the Halloween party on a whim.

She had also noticed Snow that night. The revelation sent hot tingles down her spine.

Snow was a little more evasive, but admitted that she'd noticed her too. That she and Raven had initially coined Kate Phantasm sent her into gales of laughter, and they'd yelled "Boy!" at each other for the next few minutes. Snow let on that she painted a little, pierced a lot, and was planning to try something more occupationally serious in a couple of years if she could save up the money to help her dad out while she was in school.

Left unmentioned were shapeshifting and remission.

More mystery, less history.

A second round of drinks had come, and by midnight the both of them were about laughed out. When Kate kissed her on the way back to the Corolla, warm butterflies had exploded along Snow's spine.

She was being irresponsible, she thought, to let her feelings ride her mind this way. She'd been out of control for weeks now, and this almost felt like a relapse, but this felt different somehow as well, enchanted. Part of her never wanted this to stop.

As Raven would have put it, a storm front was moving in across the cemetery.

When they reached the Corolla, Snow popped the locks and wrenched open the passenger door. Kate slid in, amused at the gallantry as Snow gently shut the door and walked around the car, getting in the driver's seat. When Snow turned over the ignition, Kate placed a hand on her knee.

"You know, the night doesn't have to be over." She said it with a wry smile, as if she could read Snow's mind. "There's this cool lookout in Washington Park we could check out. I mean, if you're up for it."

The words *Washington Park* were a bucket of ice water. Kate must have seen it cross her face. "What's wrong?"

Washington Park? What a coincidence!

That's where I drag all my victims!

Snow didn't lead with that, but only slipped her own hand over Kate's knee. Another batch of tingles shot deliciously through her. "My place isn't that far away. We could go back there."

Kate nodded. Something playful but serious flashed behind her bright green eyes, and she leaned towards Snow.

The window exploded inward.

There was a rattling boom.

The fractal events moved too fast for her mind to register, much less sequence, even as the red cloud bloomed from Kate's left cheek and the woman slumped against her like a clipped marionette. A sticky red warmth spattered against Snow's lips.

A loop began playing behind her eyes. The tiny circle appearing in the window. Glass hurtling inward. A part of Kate's scalp lifting beneath that gorgeous red hair. The spatter of crimson as something erupted from her cheek.

Kate slumping.

Kate falling.

Kate--

Mustache leaned in through the passenger side window. The left side of his face was a mass of red scabs orbiting a black eyepatch. In one hand was a dark box. It took her a moment to recognize it as a gun.

He gave her a wave.

The icy needle wove in an infernal conflagration, even before she heard the glass breaking behind her, wanting nothing more than to change, to destroy, to pierce his skull and drink his blood and tear his carcass to bloody ribbons. She wanted to feel the agony enclose her, cut her off from the rest of the world and the horrible empty space taking root within her. She wanted to feel the full shock of her body boiling into something horrible.

Nothing happened.

A sticky warmth was seeping out against her chest. Snow tried again to change, plunging the needle through her mind again and again.

All the while she howled, an ululation of anguish and horror that knew neither words nor mercy. Snow was still screaming as the cloth covered her mouth and the overpowering scent of ether ripped into her lungs. Everything went silent for a moment, then her mind rewound the last fifteen seconds. Again. Again.

She feared the loop would go on and on, over and over and over, until infinity collapsed and the stars burnt out.

Snow tried to change.

Nothing happened.

And the world went dark.

PELT

Waking up in strange places had become nothing new to Snow. Still, the cold iron beneath her was a first.

A cascade of images pounded through her mind like a punch to the stomach, and for a moment she couldn't breathe as the horrors of the night before replayed themselves.

Kate--

Rising to her knees, Snow tried not to move too fast. Her temples throbbed as if she were experiencing the worst hangover of her life and had decided to compound it with a skull fracture.

She had no idea where she was.

The room was narrow and dimly lit. One heavy door stood partly ajar at the far end of it, and the floor was old brick, cracked and uneven as if by a century's rough settling. The walls were painted wood, shoddy and peeling with moisture damage, and the roof was little more than exposed beams.

She was in an iron cage, complete with bars and steel floor, a relic from an ancient circus. Someone had stripped her down, trading her t-shirt and jeans for an amorphous black robe. She was dressed like a teenage cultist, nude beneath the uncomfortable cloth, and the thought of hands groping her naked body made her flesh burn.

Mounted on the walls were exotic trophies. She thought she recognized a massive bear, a leopard, something that may have been a moose. Surrounding her was a pervasive smell, wet and somehow feral. There were other animals nearby.

It was not a comforting thought.

Snow heard footsteps from beyond the door, starting from a long way off, reverberating against stone for what felt like forever.

There was a certain gloom, a weight above her that reminded her of a tour she and Raven had taken a couple of years ago of the Shanghai Tunnels beneath Old Town Portland. While the name had sounded mysterious and a little sexy, it had really just been the basement beneath an old restaurant that had decided to raise some extra cash. She'd looked it up later, twenty dollars the poorer, and found out that the old tunnels meant to help the river runoff beneath the city after two disastrous floods had all been boarded up almost a century ago, now partitioned into basements beneath the blocks and blocks of buildings and long since forgotten. One of them had even been turned into a bar, which admittedly would have been a better use for her twenty.

This had the same feel. Underground, with the muted echoes suggesting earth and timber surrounding her instead of walls.

No one is going to be able to hear you.

She chased the thought away as the footsteps drew close. Panic wasn't going to get her anywhere. Even shifting wouldn't help. All she could do was find a weakness, then exploit it.

Then burn this place to the ground.

As she was entertaining thoughts of arson, the door opened smoothly upon its hinges.

Mustache stepped inside, a white t-shirt stretched across his bulk and dressed in camouflage green fatigue pants. With his new eyepatch and host of fresh scars, he looked like a low-rent pirate as he folded his arms and braced one side of the entrance. Tim followed him in holding a long orange stick of plastic, looking a little embarrassed to be there, and took the other.

With both of them in short sleeves, the Liberty's Legion sunbursts on their forearms were plainly visible.

The last man through the door was Reich, looking dapper as ever in his pressed black suit. The overhead light gleamed off of his freshly shaved head, and his trimmed black beard gave him the appearance of a crossroads demon who should have had a guitar clutched in one hand and lured old blues players to their deaths. He studied her imperiously and smiled as the two shut the door behind him.

"Welcome to the real meeting." He grinned, showing all his teeth. "What are you?"

"Why?" She had meant to ask *where*, but the word forced itself out.

"Why? Why what? Why you?"

"Why *Kate*." There was a growl in her voice she hadn't expected, and the first tingle of ice slipped down her spine. For once, she had no interest in fighting the change. Something inside her was aflame. Immolation would be more than welcome.

"My dear, no one can say we didn't try alternative methods. Captain Hank's face and the homemade chloroform can attest to that."

Mustache growled, but Reich paid him no mind. "But ever the flitting butterfly, you kept slipping through our fingers. Draconian steps had to be taken. I'm sure you understand."

He snapped his fingers. Tim stepped forward, checking something on the orange stick as he did so. A flicker of lightning coursed between the two points on its end.

Reich tutted. "She was a pretty thing, but the world is full of them. Take you, for example. What are you?"

Snow didn't have time to scream as Tim jabbed the prong into her ribs. It was a wave of agony, a trace of liquid fire sent coursing through her veins. Her muscles flailed, every nerve heading in a different direction in an effort to retreat, and her jaw clacked down across her tongue as she collapsed onto the hard metal floor.

The doctor tilted his head. "Are you familiar with the psychologist John B. Watson?"

A chill that had nothing to do with the change crept through her. Raising herself up on one elbow, she spat a wad of blood upon the bricks. "Fuck off."

"I'm going to make your life very simple." Reich smiled and folded his hands together. "Some people would thank me for it. Behave, and you will feel no pain. Misbehave? You'll get the stick."

Mustache hit a button on his phone, and a shrill, high-pitched noise whirred through the air. Tim pressed his arm through the bars and hit her with the cattle prod again.

She was already on all fours, so she didn't have far to fall. Suffering spasms racked her frame, nerve endings frying as she writhed and bucked against the floor.

"Again." Reich might have been picking up his dry cleaning.

Mustache touched the control. The whirring tone echoed until it felt like her teeth would be shaken loose. Snow tried to scamper out of range. Tim stabbed her with the prod.

The anguish lasted much longer. When it was over, it

took an eternity before her fingers and toes could return the frantic signals from her brain. A rich, coppery taste was filling her mouth, and everything smelled of burnt air. Spitting another wad of blood, Snow got to her knees warily, keeping her eyes on the orange wand. "What do you want?"

"By the time we're done, you'll be pissing yourself the moment you hear that tone. Do you doubt me?" The man in the suit raised an eyebrow. Snow said nothing, and he continued. "If there was a way to peel away your human side, I would. I have no use for you as a person. Only the animal has any value to me. What are you?"

"Why?"

Reich ignored her. He only reached into his pocket, withdrew a folded piece of paper, and tossed it. It landed neatly between the bars.

With a weight pressing down in her stomach, Snow reached down and plucked it from the steel floor.

It was a picture of her from the shoulders up. Of course she recognized it.

With her two thousand dollars, she'd sent it a lifetime ago.

"Liberty's Legion is dedicated to preserving the American way of life." Reich clasped his hands together. "But preservation requires capital. Enterprise. And, I ask you, what's more apple-pie than the free market?"

Snow could barely hear him. The room lilted on its axis as her mind retreated.

Reich folded his hands. "Human trafficking. Extortion. Murder for hire. The wheels of patriotism are greased by the blood of the unclean."

She had set all this in motion.

Of course she had.

"Patrick was a lot of things. A family man, a patriot, a murderous were-coyote. But his blood was pure. There are worse among us."

There was a dutiful laugh from Tim. Mustache only glowered at Snow.

"When he didn't come back from your appointment and the other bitch was dead, it didn't take a rocket surgeon to figure out what might have happened. Or that you were now infected." Reich smiled. "You don't quite strike me as a coyote, though. No matter. As you might have guessed from Transformations, we are always shopping for new weres."

Snow didn't say anything. She felt sick to her stomach.

"I appreciate your silence. It's a fine characteristic in a woman. Frankly, it's only going to make you more valuable."

The man in the dark suit spread his hands wide, showing his teeth. "This is our Menagerie. And you're not alone."

Snow backed up to the far end of the cage, conscious of both the cattle prod and the iron bars pressing through the robe's thin material. In his element at last, Reich was simply letting the mask fall to the floor. What she saw now might have been her first real monster.

"You're here to serve. In any and every way possible. Use your imagination."

"I'm going to get out of here." She said it evenly, though the open wound of Kate's death was still a crevasse threatening to swallow her whole. "Then I'm going to rip you apart."

"Like you did Travis." Reich shrugged. "I will admit, it was a mistake to send him alone, but we didn't think you'd realized your full potential yet. To be fair, though, Travis wasn't exactly the A-team. Wherever did you hide his body?"

Snow kept her tongue.

The bald man didn't seem to mind. "It shouldn't surprise a young woman that there are some very, very--eccentric men out there, with, shall we say, nuanced tastes. People with both the money and resources to have exhausted what simple pleasures their own specie may provide."

"You're sick."

"I'm providing a service. For a very select clientele." Reich looked indignant. "Is the hunter sick? The biologist? The zookeeper? Don't be naive. People will pursue their own interests. People will collect, regardless if a legal means is available or not. Left to their own devices, who knows what deviances they may commit?"

Mustache grinned. "And who wouldn't want to fuck a hundred and thirty pound meerkat?"

"Damn it, Hank. I'm trying to make a point here." Reich shook his head. "In the Menagerie, our select clientele have a constant variety of willing and unusual partners, who admittedly turn into giant animals. The funds funnel upwards to our political wing, and those dollars buy guns. Cops. State representatives."

"We are Legion. And we are growing."

"But libertines are a fickle lot. Always looking for new extremes. New pleasures. And so the Menagerie has to keep its numbers swelling in order to accommodate them."

"You think I'm going to go along with this?" Snow was surprised by how calm she sounded.

"As you? No. Absolutely not. Frankly, your skinny ass would be just about as appealing to them as a bicycle seat. Less, even. They got tired of you in the eighth grade. But what you can become--" Reich grinned again, showing all his teeth. "--is a new experience, in a world increasingly devoid of them."

Snow started to say something, but he cut her off. "This isn't voluntary. When I leave, Hank and Tim are going to continue some lessons in negative stimulus that I find distasteful. Still, sometimes things have to be broken before you can build them anew."

"Do your part, and you'll have food. Water. Drugs. You'll live. Try to get cute, or try to starve yourself out--" The bald man tapped the near wall. Her eyes drew upward to the skins adorning them, the dried out husks of weathered fur. "We also do a brisk business in pelts."

Reich stepped out into the hallway and snapped his fingers. Tim shut the door behind him.

Mustache started forward, a hungry look in his one good eye.

"You know what they say about payback?"

Snow did.

✵

EVERY INCH OF HER ACHED. IT DIDN'T SEEM RIGHT THAT SHE could absorb that sheer volume of punishment and stay conscious, but her battered body remained as awake as ever.

Piercing tone. Shock. Piercing tone. Shock. Over and over, over and over, until the pair of them had gotten tired of using the prod and started using their boots, their fists. Mustache in particular had quite a bit of rage to work out, and as the blows had rained down, she was ashamed to remember that she'd begged them to stop. There had only been the pain, and the tone. The pain, and the tone.

At the end, her robe had ridden up, her nude form a collection of bloody gashes, scorch marks, and bruises. For a moment, she thought the beating would progress, but Mustache had almost prissily pulled the amorphous garment back down to cover her. "In your dreams, bitch. Your kind disgust me."

He'd punctuated every word with a kick and the tone. Her ribs must have broken, for each breath she now drew was a raspy tear.

Only when they'd grown tired had they thrown her back into the cage and locked it behind her. She'd hit the iron bars in back with a jarring thud, and only then had her consciousness allowed her to wander.

Snow ran a tongue over her torn lips. She wasn't sure how much time had passed, but all her teeth seemed to still be accounted for. More concerning was the swollen flesh around both her eyes and the way her vision had tapered to thin slits at best.

Every move was an exercise in anguish. She forced herself to sit up against the far wall, her back pressing against the cold bars. Snow thought about her father, Raven, Talbot, even Duke. Thought about remaining in a hell they'd never know she'd visited, days into months, months into years.

She had no doubt that the Legion could get away with it. Hadn't people always in the past? Yesterday she'd had her whole life in front of her. Today she was only property, something to be used and then discarded.

Again, and again.

For just a moment, she wished that the coyote had finished the job.

Two thousand dollars doesn't buy quality control.

But that was weakness. And if there was one thing she had learned in the last few weeks, it was that weakness could be melted away.

The dark bloom in her skull, if it was still there, might end her at any moment.

What was a cage to that?

All she had was now. All she had was herself.

And it was all she needed.

Snow tested the bars. The iron door rattled on its old hinges, but didn't budge. Despite the boasts, the Menagerie wasn't doing so well that it could afford anything past the Ringling Brothers' heyday, but the bars were still sufficient. She wasn't going anywhere, at least not as Snow.

She pushed away her guilt, pushed away her father,

pushed away everything but herself. Calming down, her mind full of focus, she saw the needle. A chill coursed through her.

Concentrate on being your best self.

Your human self.

Fuck that.

CARAPACE

When the glacier slammed into her, Snow reveled in the pain.

Her limbs spasmed boneless as she writhed on the floor, organs and veins gelatinizing into meaty gum. Her skull collapsed into a shapeless mass of tissue, and broken ribs dissolved into so much flotsam as extra limbs galvanized themselves, ripping from her torso in an explosion of flailing flesh that hurt worse than anything she'd felt so far. When her torso dwindled into almost nothing at all, her head lengthened, extending from the crown like a fleshy balloon.

She rode the agony now, not transcending but simply accepting it. There could be nothing worthwhile without sacrifice.

At the end, she found herself splayed across the steel floor. Snow was parched with thirst.

Her gelatinous form pressed against the bars, as pliable now as pudding. Compressed, her bulky form tested the exposed space and then prodded it, squeezing itself through an inch at a time, yanking her head through slowly like a balloon through a tube. When she finally popped free, her thirst had grown deeper, and she realized with growing alarm that she couldn't breathe. With a speed she didn't know she could muster, Snow clambered on her tentacles across the broken stones to the wooden door.

Wrapping a tentacle around the latch, she pushed. Nothing.

From her lower vantage point, she offered the door a cursory examination. There was a round inch of space in the center of the door, a peephole with which to check on prisoners.

Conscious of how little air remained in her system, Snow forced herself to relax.

This was going to hurt.

She measured the opening with a predator's eye, then thrust a tentacle through the gap. The effect was not unlike shoving a sock full of ground beef through a keyhole. There was resistance, and it was gross, but eventually it was going to force itself through.

The first tentacle through the gap, she pressed another, and then another. The boneless appendages compressed and then flowed fluidly through the minimal space until they found purchase on the other side.

If someone was to come along now, Snow had no doubt that this would be the end of her. No one could put octopi in a corner, and she had legitimate questions as to the market for the gummy monstrosity she now found herself as.

Tentacles writhing in a fleshy blossom of flora, her puckered limbs found purchase on the other side of the door and heaved, wrenching her body through the gap. Her vision buckled, beak clacking against the cheap wood, but her amorphous core slowly slipped through the aperture. Light dwindled to mere pinpoints as her head collapsed, her respiration growing shallower and shallower.

For a moment she thought it wouldn't work, that her air

would run out and she'd be forced to change back, the door neatly bisecting her skull.

Then she was through with a liquid pop, reappearing as a nightmare seed in the stone hallway as her head ballooned back into its natural shape. Instinct sent her scrambling up the wall, each writhing tentacle adhering to the porous wood as a light sparkled around the corner. Footsteps sent vibrations to every quivering mouth.

Snow pressed herself into the void where wall met ceiling, lightheaded as her air supply tapered away. She waited for the light to draw closer.

When the mustached figure stepped beneath her to look through the door, they didn't so much as glance up in her direction. Snow was a colorless ball of protoplasm, buried in the shadows.

She felt, rather than heard, the tone.

Snow plummeted from the ceiling in a silent cannonball of flesh. Her body struck the crown of Hank's head with an audible splat, and the big man let out a shriek of surprise as her puckering tentacles wrapped around his face, latching to his flesh with a noisome sucking sound.

Even ambushed, Mustache was fast. His hands dug into her elongated head as he attempted to wrench her away, veins standing out in stark relief against his beefy forearms.

But his two arms against her eight was never going to be a fair fight. He might as well have been wrestling raw muscle as her weight pressed down, filling his nose, his mouth. His beating hands began to lose their momentum and strength as they degraded into cheap flails.

Clacking her beak, Snow drove herself through his other eye.

✳

THE OCTOPUS WAS HUNGRY BUT DYING, AND FOR A MOMENT Snow wrestled with it for control.

She was aware of how easy it would be to start pecking morsels off of Hank. To press further through the socket of his eye, taking tasty bites of the raw grey candy therein until she suffocated on dry land. It was what she deserved, after all.

A predator demands its prey.

But if she gave in, all would be lost. Even if she didn't asphyxiate, no one would show restraint dealing with an engorged octopus full of human sauce.

She found the center, the cold needle in her mind. With a physical grunt, she punched it through.

Snow felt herself ice over.

A dark chill seemed to lick at her exposed flesh, her raw nerve endings searing as bones reasserted themselves out of her jellied meat, her organs redefining themselves into the predominant core. The shift hurt, to be sure, but it was nothing compared to the initial change.

This was her body, the one she had spent years building and perfecting. She resumed it in a matter of seconds.

It felt like coming home.

Rolling off of the mustachioed corpse, Snow hurtled down the hallway, trying to stick close to the walls, her two legs feeling phantom and unreal. She had a sense that the host of other forms were still with her, only a siren song away.

Everywhere there were rich animal scents, fecund odors wafting from beneath the other doors in their hasty wooden partitions. Bestial noises mixed with human sobs, all wailing or howling in the darkness.

There were doors everywhere, but she only wanted one. And it was wide open.

Light spilled from the threshold. Snow smelled the smoke first, a rich musk against the reek of wet masonry. Reich and an older gentleman with a hundred dollar haircut were huddled around a table, the red flares of their cigar ends bright coronas against the low light. In front of them were two tumblers of Scotch and a pair of ledgers. A nude woman sat listlessly in a wooden chair by the far wall, leaning on a beaten filing cabinet. The glassy look in her eyes spoke of either heavy drugs or a frontal lobotomy. She'd been made just part of the furniture.

Currency was everywhere. Snow could see it in verdant stacks on the desk, filling cardboard cartons by the near wall. Grocery sacks bulged with tattered green. But the men paid no attention to this, only the figures scrawled across the page, the older man snapping something quick and cutting that Reich nodded along to immediately.

For the first time, she thought of how truly ramshackle the entire operation was. The partitioned wall to her left had been thrown together from badly painted plywood. The doors themselves had been salvaged, no two alike, and inexpertly hinged into place. Even the hanging bulbs looked haphazardly strung, and they were almost certainly a fire hazard.

For all the grand words and declarations of nobility, this was a facade. These were no architects, no builders of a grand design. They were little boys, playing naughty in their parent's basement.

A hot flare of anger caught inside her and burned.

Kate dead, and how many others? For what?

The wave of ice struck her almost at once, somehow not extinguishing the rage but only doubling down, then tripling, a glacier slipping into first gear.

She bit down on her lower lip, welcoming the change this time, riding it, accepting the agony within herself as her skin hardened into grey pebble and new legs erupted from her abdomen.

The anguish was nothing compared to what she wanted to dish out.

Snow felt her skull retreat into her body, her eyes becoming beady and black. Her fingers were elongating and flowing together, sharpening into swollen stones. She snapped them together in razored eloquence. One was a neat, prissy pair of bladed bones, the other a massive scissor half the size of her whole body. She wondered as to the miracle of nature that could allow such a creature to balance itself without simply dragging one limb behind it like a barbarian with an axe.

If they heard the clacking of her thin legs against the cobbles, they gave no sign.

Scuttling through the doorway, she was halfway to the desk before either man could be bothered to turn around. Even as a decapod, Snow recognized the look of patronizing annoyance on the older man's face, the *grown-up's-are-talking* sneer that passed for command.

Snow took his head off with one clean stroke.

Reich's mouth kept moving for a moment, his deferent explanation apparently more pressing than the hot gout of blood that jetted across his features. The old man's head bounced against the hardwood desk once, cigar still clenched in its teeth and pinwheeling gore. It skidded off the edge and into the paper sacks lining the partition wall.

The woman in the corner gave no sign that she was still on the material plane, much less that a crab monster was running amok.

With her little claw, Snow hoisted herself up onto the chair and then the desk, knocking the gushing body to one side. Reich shook his head and managed to come to his senses, scrambling back and away from the armored behemoth, kicking over his chair before rolling to one side. His hand flinched into his coat, and he yanked out a small plastic box that seemed significant to Snow.

From the corner of her eyestalk, she watched a little red cherry begin to blossom in the grocery bag. She thought she could spot the first faint vestiges of smoke.

Then Reich was jamming his index finger at the plastic box, thrusting it over and over again at a rubber button. For the first time, the woman in the corner reacted, putting her hands to her ears and appearing to howl, baring her teeth in a nightmare, jaw-splitting rictus. Even the bald man was gritting his teeth.

As she plunged over the hardwood and scuttled back down onto the bricks, Snow realized that Reich's lips were moving, spilling out a frenetic dance of epithets and curses and prayers. For her part, Snow heard nothing but the blood pulsing in her carapace.

As she would later discover, crabs don't have ears.

Reich's back hit the wall, and he fumbled around for a weapon, any weapon. He snatched up a coat rack in the corner and tried to piston it at Snow's face, but one swipe from her massive claw set it recoiling in splinters. Rolling away from the grasping pincer, Reich tumbled across the partition wall, found his feet, and plunged his hand into the filing cabinet.

It came out with a shiny, nickel-plated device that Snow dully recognized even as she fell upon the cornered man. Pointing it downward, Reich's mouth yawned in a silent scream as he pulled the trigger. The little thing barked fire, and Snow was aware of a burning pain blossoming in her abdomen as several holes ripped through her carapace.

Leaking gore, she swung the behemoth claw between the bald man's legs, scissoring it around Reich's groin in a funereal embrace of bone and chitin.

With pure animal instinct, she clamped down.

His mouth opened in a paroxysm of horror and pain, even as his pelvis bisected and the front of the claw tore a deep furrow through his gut. A torrent of scarlet sprayed from his mouth as Snow readjusted her grip and cleaved again.

And again.

And again.

She was dimly aware that her strength was leaving her. A thin blue substance poured freely from her cracked shell, puddling onto the old masonry beneath her. The room was quickly becoming an icebox.

Reich was prostrate where he fell, unmoving.

Snow cut into him again.

✵

THE GLACIER WAS ALL AROUND HER.

As the light blackened her vision dwindled to a single dark speck. This was what she had wanted since the beginning. The way out.

Wasn't it?

Her father would be taken care of. No more changes. No more worries. Only emptiness, and the abyss beyond.

Everything would be solved.

So little time in which to be undone.

So why did this feel like failure?

Consciousness fading away, one of Snow's final thoughts was of the frozen needle.

With the last of her strength, she stabbed it home.

SKIN

When she came to, the building was on fire.

The first thing she was aware of was the smoke. Flames licked up the partition walls, most of the ill-gotten funds the Legion had produced doubling as kindling. Whatever low-rent paint they'd used was apparently the cosmetic equivalent of lighter fluid.

Snow's hands traced across her abdomen. Her fingers made out the barest white circles, three of them just beneath her right rib. They were the merest suggestion of the gaping exit wounds that had been there minutes before.

For just a moment, she thought she remembered an empty plateau stretching on to nothingness, and then tucked it away forever.

She wondered how close she'd come to dying.

As it was, Snow was starving. White spots danced across her vision as she lurched to her feet, the room swaying and bucking as if she'd found herself at sea.

Of the woman in the corner, there was no sign. Over the crackling of the flames, Snow thought she could hear the clack of hooves beat down the hallway.

The sound chilled her. She wasn't sure why.

Reich was lying in pieces at her feet, cold blue eyes staring both into the ceiling and nothing at all. She ransacked his pockets, but all she turned up was a wallet and a wicked-looking pocketknife. No keys.

Snow glanced around the room, time already running out. It was hard to think straight, the smoke already beginning to collect by the ceiling. It seared her lungs with each gasping breath.

Plucking a black trench coat from the shattered rack, she slipped it over her shoulders and began rifling through the desk. They had to be here somewhere, didn't they?

When the smoke had grown too thick and the drawers had all turned up empty, Snow had started for the door, imagining running through the burning building and just trying to kick open every door.

The keys hung on a hook just inside the entrance, a massive ring reminiscent of some medieval jailor.

Boys playing at cops and robbers.

She grabbed them and was halfway down the hallway before she paused and went back into the office.

Snow was only human, after all.

❄

AT THE EDGE OF THE MT HOOD NATIONAL FOREST, SNOW parked the Corolla, got out, and sat against the hood.

She'd taken her time to find an area that was as far away from houses and suburbia as she could manage. The freshly packed gym bag was in the trunk, and she tucked her set of keys into a small box magnetically affixed beneath the bumper. Like any good scout, it turned out the key to being a monster was to be prepared.

Snow and a dozen others had spilled out of the burning

basement at a little past three in the morning, smoke billowing from the lower windows of the old warehouse and the crackling oranges flames clearly visible against the dirty glass. Sirens were already blaring nearer, and most of the others had raced off across the parking lot and into the night without a word or a glance back in her direction. Snow didn't mind at all. The fewer people who remembered her face, the better.

There wasn't a were amongst them who wanted to be there when the cops arrived.

Snow had jogged a few blocks over before hailing a cab. The befuddled driver had eyed her warily, a sleek, barely dressed thing that had slipped into his backseat with edges sharp enough to cut bone. His constant glances through the rearview mirror were initially curious until he'd angled them towards her chest. A sharp bark and the driver had hoisted his gaze away, suddenly all business and his eyes on the road.

She thought that from now on she might be having that effect on people.

Raven had been huddled on the loveseat when Snow had wandered in through the front door, eyes red and running. Apparently the shooting had made the local news two days ago, and the raccoon punk had been holding a vigil with Talbot ever since. She'd leapt up the moment Snow stepped inside, wrapping her up in a bear hug that could have cracked bone. Talbot danced around the pair of them in a frantic tarantella, his little pink tongue yipping merrily away. There were tears and recriminations, but most of all there was hope.

Hope that the Legion would fall apart. Hope that the dark bloom in her head would stay dormant. Hope that she had finally found a little breathing room in a world without much of it to spare.

And if it didn't, she would face that too.

The lined pockets of the trench coat didn't hurt. Nor did the two grocery bags full of cash even now resting on her kitchen table.

The head of the hiking trail was only a dozen yards away, and Snow took it, her cheap flip-flops smacking against the gravel. The night air was already chilly going on cold, but she knew she didn't need more than the cheap t-shirt and sweats that she was already thinking of as her shredding clothes.

The boulder was at the first major turn in the trail, a graceful arc that led up and in towards the deeper woods. Snow climbed atop it and waited for the change to take her.

She looked up at the moon, a yellow sliver of bone, and counted the stars.

As the glacier coursed down her spine, she knew what she would be.

✳

ACKNOWLEDGMENTS

Many thanks go out to the following, whose support has taken on an ever-varying array of forms: Sam Richard at Weirdpunk for making this book possible, Carlton Mellick III and Rose O' Keefe at Eraserhead for taking a chance on me in the first place, Pete Kahle at Bloodshot Books for what must come after, Mike Deich for the body-piercing expertise (any mistakes are completely my own, and should not impugn the finest man to ever put a hole in you), Jan Juliani, who has suffered so many of these to their unmerciful fates, and, finally, my most heartfelt thanks to my partner, Cecily, for her infinite, unshifting patience through everything.

ABOUT THE AUTHOR

Roland Blackburn is a father, IPA enthusiast, and author of *The Flesh Molder's Love Song* and the upcoming *Marmalade*. He lives in Troutdale, Oregon with his wife, two children, and multiple dogs. After a rough night out on the moors, he's proud that his assumption of the human form is nearly complete.

ALSO BY WEIRDPUNK BOOKS

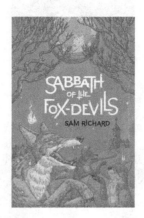

Sabbath of the Fox-Devils by Sam Richard

After learning about the existence of a powerful grimoire through a cartoon, 12-year-old Joe is determined to find it and change his lot in life. But in doing so, he'll also uncover a local priest's dark secret and how it may be connected to Joe's brother abruptly leaving town five years ago.

Part homage to the small-creature horror films of the 80s (*Ghoulies, Gremlins, The Gate*) and part Splatterpunk take on a Goosebumps book, *Sabbath of the Fox-Devils* is a weird, diabolical coming-of-age horror story of self-liberation in an oppressive religious environment set during the Satanic Panic. Prepare your soul to revel in the darkness.

"Light the black candles and invert the cross as Sam Richard conjures a coming-of-age story of Satanic panic, creature carnage, and blasphemous terror!"

— RYAN HARDING (*GENITAL GRINDER, HEADER 3*)

The Mud Ballad - Jo Quenell

NEVER BE ALONE AGAIN

In a dying railroad town, a conjoined twin wallows in purgatory for the murder of his brother. A disgraced surgeon goes to desperate ends to reconnect with his lost love. When redemption comes with a dash of black magic, the two enter a world of talking corpses, flesh-eating hogs, rude mimes, and ritualistic violence.

"Jo Quenell's debut novella explores both regret and connection in the weirdest and wildest ways possible. Good times!"

— DANGER SLATER, AUTHOR OF THE WONDERLAND AWARD WINNING *I WILL ROT WITHOUT YOU*

The New Flesh: A Literary Tribute to David Cronenberg - Edited by Sam
Richard and Brendan Vidito

Videodrome. Scanners. The Brood. Crash. The Fly. The films of David
Cronenberg have haunted and inspired generations. His name has
become synonymous with the body horror subgenere and the term
"Cronenbergian" has been used to describe the stark, grotesque, and
elusive quality of his work. These eighteen stories bring his themes
and ideas into the present, throbbing with unnatural life.

A Splatterpunk Awards nominee for Best Anthology, The New Flesh
features stories by Brain Evenson, Gwendolyn Kiste, Cody
Goodfellow, Katy Michelle Quinn, Ryan Harding, and more. Plus an
introduction by the legendary Kathe Koja!